story which brings the war vividly to life.

JULIA ECCLESHARE

*It's a short read but one that has a strong impact and stays in
your head even after you've finished, ensuring that* Valentine

A MESSAGE FROM CHICKEN HOUSE

The point of this brilliant, poignant, funny and exciting story is that the chance to play and enjoy sport shouldn't ever be restricted by gender or anything else. (After all, both my daughters are better at football than me!) This is the real-life story of how women's football began – mixed with some perfect passes from a world of what might have happened next. Quick, Rebecca – on my head! Goal power!

BARRY CUNNINGHAM
Publisher
Chicken House

LILY *and the* ROCKETS

Rebecca Stevens

Chicken House

2 PALMER STREET, FROME, SOMERSET BA11 1DS

Text © Rebecca Stevens 2019
Illustrations © Harriet Taylor Seed 2019

First published in Great Britain in 2019
Chicken House
2 Palmer Street
Frome, Somerset BA11 1DS
United Kingdom
www.chickenhousebooks.com

Cover & interior design by Steve Wells
Cover & interior illustrations by Harriet Taylor Seed
Typeset by Dorchester Typesetting Group Ltd
Printed and bound in Great Britain by CPI Group (UK) Ltd, Croydon, CR0 4YY

The paper used in this Chicken House book is made from wood
grown in sustainable forests.

1 3 5 7 9 10 8 6 4 2

British Library Cataloguing in Publication data available.

ISBN 978-1-912626-12-0
eISBN 978-1-912626-25-0

Lily and the Rockets was inspired by
The Gerty Naylor Show, *which was written and
performed by my friend Tony Haase.
I'd like to thank him for letting me use his
original idea for my story.*

Also by Rebecca Stevens

Valentine Joe
Rose in the Blitz

PART ONE

Woolwich, South London
Summer 1917

CHAPTER ONE

Oh, I remember that day. Me and Amy May, Amy May and me, lying in the grass on Plumstead Marshes, the sun on our faces and the world at our feet. We'd left school that afternoon, finished for ever, and we felt that anything was possible.

We were fourteen and we'd been best friends since time began.

'What would you do, Lily Dodd,' Amy May was saying, 'if you could have any job in the world?'

That was easy.

'Goalkeeper,' I said.

'That's not a job,' said Amy. 'Playing football. It's a hobby. Something you do with your dad in the park after school. You don't get paid for it.'

'Dad used to get paid,' I said. 'Playing for the works' team.'

'How much?'

'I don't know! It was before I was born, when him and Mum were courting. She used to go and watch him, down at the old Manor Ground. He said she liked looking at his legs.'

Mum had died when I was little, so I didn't know much about her. Only what Dad told me and what I could imagine from looking at the oval photograph that hung above the piano in the front room, with her sitting on a velvet chair with a sort of painted ruin behind her, looking like she was trying not to laugh.

'It's different though, Lil,' said Amy. 'Your dad ... well ... *he's a man*.'

'That is true,' I said, sitting up and flaring my nostrils like Miss Hogweed, our teacher at school. 'A lot of people are men, Amy May. Half the human race, in fact. Stupid!'

For some reason, this made us laugh and laugh. And when we'd stopped laughing, Amy said, 'And you're a girl.'

'Yes,' I said. 'I am a girl. A very tall girl who is

very good at football. And you, Amy May,' I said, doing the teacher voice again, 'are a very silly girl with a very bad attitude.'

She gave me a little slap. 'Ha!' she said. 'No more Miss Hogweed for us! No nay never! No nay never no moooooore . . .'

I joined in and we both sang at the top of our voices: 'Will I play the wild rover, no never, no more!'

'No more lessons, no more learning, won't be long before we're earning!' added Amy.

I flopped back on to the grass. 'You did say I could choose any job in the world.'

'True.'

'So, I choose goalkeeper.' I knew it couldn't happen, of course. Girls couldn't be goalkeepers, not professional ones. They could hardly even play football in the park without boys shouting things at them and old ladies shaking their heads. I just liked saying it, so I said it again. 'I want. To be. A goalkeeper.'

'Why?'

Most people grow out of saying 'Why?' all the time when they're three years old. Amy May never did. Some people said she was a nosy parker, but I thought it was nice. She just wanted to know about everything, which is a good thing in my opinion.

'Because it's the best,' I said. 'Best position on the pitch, Dad says. It's all quiet at first and lonely. You stand in your goal, watching the game, willing your boys to score, waiting, waiting. Then all of a sudden, when you least expect it, they lose the ball, the other team's coming towards your goal, your boys chasing them, but they won't catch up, you know it, they know it, you're their last chance, the man with the ball gets past your defenders, you look him in the eye, you know he's going to shoot, he hesitates for one second – one second only – he kicks, he shoots, the ball comes at you, whoaaahhhhhh . . . and you save it. And you, you are the hero, Amy May. You.'

Amy had stopped listening. When I said she was interested in everything that wasn't quite true. She always turned off when I started talking about football.

'What about you?' I said. 'If you could have any job in the world, what would you do?'

Amy thought for a second. 'A singer,' she said. 'In a travelling theatre troupe, going all round the world, making people cry with the loveliness of my voice. When the war's over, obviously. They don't want to do any more crying at the moment. Or a dancer in pink tights.' She gasped suddenly, as if she'd been stung. 'A woman with a flower shop! That'd be a lovely job! Or a comedienne, like that whatsername we saw at the Hippodrome with your dad.'

'Vesta Tilley.'

'Yeah. She was funny.' Amy lay back and smiled at the sky. 'Perhaps I'll just be a queen . . .'

'Being a queen is not a job.'

'It's as much a job as being a goalkeeper.'

'It is not! Being a queen is just being married to a king. Which isn't a job either, by the way.'

'I don't see why. He gets paid enough.'

I picked a feathery bit of grass and chewed the end. 'My dad hates the King,' I said.

Amy was a lot more interested in that sort of thing than in football. 'Why?' she said.

'Don't know really. He hates all the royals. Leeches and spongers, he calls them. Living off the working man—'

'And woman.'

'German too, of course, all of them, German.'

'That's not their fault, poor dears.'

'True.'

'Any more than it's your fault you're daft.'

'Who are you calling daft? You're the one who wants to be a queen.'

'And you're the one who wants to be a goal-keeper.'

I didn't say anything, just leant over and tickled the inside of her nostril with the feathery bit of grass.

'Argh! Get off!' Amy flapped about with her hands, trying to grab the grass. And then, as we rolled about on the ground laughing, a shadow fell between us and the sun and we looked up to see a boy. A boy with spiky hair and a football under his arm, grinning down at us. Amy sniffed.

'What are you looking at, Billy Cracken?'

'Not you, Amy May. Want to play, Lily? You can be in goal.'

I looked at Amy. She rolled her eyes. 'Shove off, freckles,' she said. 'She doesn't want to play with you.'

I did actually, but I was scared someone might

see us out there on the marshes. Other boys from school, men going home from work at the Arsenal. They might stop and laugh, say things about girls playing football, lanky legs, stuff like that.

Amy poked Billy's leg with the toe of her boot. 'Go on, Bill. Scram!'

I liked the way she talked to boys, so funny and easy. Amy had seven brothers – three fighting in France, three working in the Arsenal making the bombs and bullets to send to the ones in France, and one younger than her, who was still at school, not making anything except trouble, her mum used to say. So she was used to it, Amy was, talking to boys. It wasn't like that for me. Since Mum died there was just me and Dad at home, though I still heard her singing round the house sometimes, at least I think it was her:

'She's my lady love, she is my dove, my baby love…'

Dad heard it too, I know he did, though he never said anything. His eyes would go all misty and he'd look up at something that wasn't there, hanging in the air in front of his face, and then he'd shake out his newspaper with a big loud crackle and start talking about football or get up and make a cup of tea. So anyway, I couldn't talk to boys, not like Amy.

I could tell Billy Cracken didn't know what to say either, so he lobbed his football down towards the ground beside our heads, trying to make us jump and scream like girls do sometimes. Quick as a flash I stuck out my arm and caught the ball with one hand before it hit the ground. I've got big hands – goalkeeper's hands, Dad always says – and right from where I was lying, I threw Billy Cracken's heavy old football way up over his head and into the brambles at the other side of the path that led down to the river.

'Oi! My ball!'

I laughed and Amy joined in. 'Go get it then, Bill!'

'Yeah, Bill! Off you go!'

As Billy Cracken struggled off grumbling into the brambles to get his ball, Amy May stopped laughing and rolled over to look me in the eye.

'Really, though, Lil. What are we going to do? We've got to find a way to earn money.'

'I don't know. Dad doesn't want me to go into service and I don't either. I can't think of anything worse, having to leave Dad and go and live in some big house over the river, up at dawn, scrubbing floors, laying fires, all that.'

'People telling you what to do all the time. Worse than school.'

'Yeah.'

For a minute we lay there, listening to the slap of the water against the riverbank as a barge drifted past, and the constant grind and roar of the machines in the Arsenal. Then Amy said, 'We could be munitionettes!'

'What?'

'You know. Apply to work at the Arsenal.'

'I know what munitionettes are, Amy.'

'They're crying out for more women workers, my brother said. With so many men gone and that.'

'We're not women, Amy,' I said. 'We're girls. You've got to be eighteen to work in munitions. We're not old enough.'

'You look old enough. Tall enough, anyhow.'

'You don't. You look about twelve.'

'Yes, but I am a very good liar.' Amy's eyes danced at me. She had the funniest eyes in the world, Amy May: one blue and one brown, like certain types of dogs. One from each parent, Amy used to say. She hated them, or pretended to, but I thought they were pretty. So did lots of people. Especially boys.

'All right,' I said. 'Let's do it.'

Amy laughed. Then she stopped laughing and looked at me. 'Do you mean it?' she said.

I stood up and held out a hand to pull her up. 'I do,' I said.

She took a deep breath. We looked at each other.

'Tomorrow, then?' she said. 'We go down the Labour Exchange? Make them give us a job?'

'Tomorrow.'

Amy reached up and patted my cheek, then poked me in the ribs and ran off, fair hair flying out behind her, away from the river, back towards the streets. I stayed where I was, watching the boats. The river was the colour of milky tea.

It was the end of something, that hot afternoon in 1917, our last day as schoolgirls. But the start of something too, I thought. Something new.

And that's when I heard the scream.

CHAPTER TWO

It was Amy. Amy, my Amy May, best friend since the beginning of time, had made this sound like I'd never heard her make before, and I was scared.

'Amy? Amy!'

She was standing near the entrance to the foot tunnel when I found her, still as a rock, staring at nothing. Her little brother Bertie was a few feet away, his face all smeared with tears and dirt, and there was a piece of paper lying on the ground between them. I could see what it was and I knew what it meant.

It was a telegram. Bertie must've brought it from home. Their mum would've sent him to find her.

'Don't touch it!' Amy's face was white. She

looked angry, her lips a thin line in her little face.

She had three brothers fighting in France. So far they'd been lucky, compared to other families. But now . . .

I bent down and read the words:

I deeply regret to inform you—

'I said, leave it!'

I'd never heard Amy so fierce, but I picked it up anyway. It was crumpled and smeared with dirt from Bertie's fingers. Before I could read it, Amy turned and ran into the entrance to the tunnel. I ran after her, the telegram in my hand. She hadn't stopped to call the lift that took you underground to the start of the tunnel and I could hear her boots clanging on the iron steps as she went down. By the time I got to the bottom she was nearly halfway along, her little figure flying through the white-tiled passageway that went under the river.

'Amy! Wait! Ameeeeee!'

When she got to the middle, she stopped dead and turned to face me. Her face was set, like it was carved out of marble, like an angel on a tomb. I took a step towards her, but without looking at me she held up one hand to stop me. Her fingers were all inky from school.

'Don't,' she said. '*Don't!*' Then, still not looking at me, she held out her hand for the telegram. When I gave it to her she tore it in half without looking at it and dropped it on the ground. 'It's Arthur,' she said. Her voice was flat. Then she gave herself a little shake. 'I left Bertie up there,' she said, then turned and walked past me back the way we'd come.

'Amy,' I said.

She stopped and, without turning round, said, 'I'm going over there.'

I looked at the back of her head. Her pretty hair curling around her neck looked all wrong. How could anything be pretty when the world was so horrible?

'That's what I'll do,' she said, turning so quickly that I had to step back. 'I'll go there.'

'What? Where, Amy?' But I knew.

'France,' she said. 'The front, where the fighting is. Wherever Arthur was. Wherever he is now.' Her eyes glittered and for a minute she looked almost excited. She tapped her mouth with one ink-stained forefinger and looked at me for the first time since she'd heard about Arthur. 'Why should they be out there all alone, Lil? He was only nineteen. It's not fair!'

Arthur was her favourite brother. She would never admit it, but I knew, because he was my favourite too. He was the second eldest, with a freckled, funny face and strong brown arms that twinkled in the sun with hundreds of tiny gold hairs. They used to fascinate me when I was little, but I wasn't little any more. I was Lily Dodd, fourteen years old, and I felt like I was a hundred.

'What about us?' I said. 'What about you and me? What about us getting jobs at the Arsenal?'

'No,' she said. 'I can't stay here, nice and safe in London, when they're out there all alone.'

I wasn't going to try and persuade her. There was no point. Once Amy May had made up her mind, nobody could change it. So I just said, 'What will you do?'

'I'll be a nurse. Just go and help. When they're wounded and that. Help them.'

I looked at her, five foot three and fourteen years old. I didn't know how old you had to be to train as a nurse, but it was bound to be older than that.

'They need volunteers,' she said, as if she knew what I was thinking. 'They're desperate. They'd take anyone.'

I didn't say anything.

'I can work!' she shouted suddenly, as if someone had said she couldn't. She looked along the length of the tunnel, the line of lights along the ceiling disappearing into nothingness.

'But—'

She held up her hand again. She knew what I was going to say. She always did.

'I'll ask Miss Hogweed. She'll tell me what to do.'

Our teacher's sister was a nurse, a proper one, who was out at the front looking after the wounded soldiers. Miss Hogweed used to read out bits of her letters in class and try not to cry. We never understood why she found them so sad, because they just described the little French town where her sister was living, the friends she'd made, things like that. She made it sound like fun.

'But—' I said it again, and again Amy interrupted.

'I know, I know, I know,' she said. 'I'm not old enough. I know. 'But,—' and her face shone as she looked at me, 'it's like I said, Lily Dodd. I am a very good liar.'

Then she pressed the button to call the lift and we waited in silence as it creaked its way down. Bertie was still there when we emerged in the glare of the afternoon, standing in the sun exactly where we'd left him, wiping the tears and snot from his face with the back of his hand. A bird was singing its stupid little song against the background throb of the Arsenal's machines and a tugboat hooted on the river. Billy Cracken had arrived and was sitting with his back against the wall, looking at us and picking the petals off a dog daisy.

Amy went over to her brother and, without a word, dropped to her knees and hugged him round the waist, rocking him in her arms. Then she got up, carefully wiped his face with the edge of her pinafore and held out her hand.

'Come on, Bertie. Let's go home.'

He took her hand and they headed off without looking back, towards the network of tiny streets where they lived, to face their mum.

And that was it. My best friend was gone. Nothing would ever be the same again.

I stood there for a bit, watching the barges with their big brown sails drifting past on the river and trying to work out what I was feeling. And then, when I found I couldn't, or whatever it was I didn't know the word for it, I turned to go home. I didn't know what else to do.

'Lil?'

I'd forgotten Billy was there. He'd got up and was standing by the wall, wiping his hands on the seat of his trousers and looking at me. I looked back at him for a minute, then shook my head. There was nothing we could say, either of us, so I turned and walked away, leaving him standing there with tears in his eyes and the petals of the dog daisy scattered round his feet. He was a nice boy, Billy Cracken, an orphan, lived in the children's home on Plumstead Road. It was him who first got me playing football with the boys. I remember the day so well. I'd been all on my own in the playground because Amy was off school with a cough, and I was crying a bit because I was cold and the other girls had been teasing me, making comments about the size of my feet and how I had to go to school in my dad's boots (which wasn't true at the time actually, I was only about seven). Billy had just bounced his ball towards where I was standing by the wall, and when I looked up he said, 'Want to play? You can be in goal if you like,' and that was it. I played with the boys every break after that, even after Amy got better.

I walked on, crossing Beresford Square, where the stallholders were packing up for the day and the air smelt of horses and fish and rotten vegetables. There was rubbish everywhere and men with barrows, heaving crates, clattering and laughing just as if it was an ordinary day and my best friend hadn't just heard that her favourite brother was dead. They shouted at me as I walked past, like they always did. It wasn't their fault. They didn't know what had happened and that I was feeling a feeling I didn't have a name for.

'Oi! Lanky legs! What's the weather like up there?' I got that one a lot. The boy who shouted looked younger than me and had a pinched white face.

Then, another voice: 'I'd give you a kiss if I had a ladder!'

That one I'd never heard before. I thought it was quite funny actually. I liked the thought of the little man who sold whelks from a barrel leaning a ladder up against me and climbing up to give me a kiss. I didn't mind the shouting, not usually. It was just when I was playing football with Dad or Billy Cracken, when they laughed at me and put me off my game, then I hated it. It made me angry in a way I didn't understand.

Everything looked the same when I got home and opened the front door of the little house in Spray Street. The hallway was cool and dark after the sunshine outside, and smelt like it always did, of damp and soot and kippers. Mum would be looking down from her place over the piano in the front room, and Dad would be on the stairs lacing up his boots ready for work. He was working nights at the Arsenal that summer, which meant I spent my evenings alone, but I didn't mind. I'd have an egg for my tea, or a bit of cold pie, and then go out and kick a ball against the wall in the back alley until it got too dark to see, and then I'd go to bed. And in the morning, Dad would be there, smelling of oil and grinning at me through the dirt.

He was grinning now as I walked in.

'Hey ho, Lily-oh,' he said. 'How was your last day at school?'

And then he saw my face.

'Lil?' He got up from his chair and went over to where I was standing in the doorway. 'What's happened, girl? What is it?'

My eyes prickled, but I decided I wasn't going to cry, even though it would've been nice to bury my face in the shoulder of his scratchy old jacket and breathe in its familiar musty smell of wool and tobacco. I suddenly knew what I was going to do. Amy might be going to France to be a nurse but I could do my bit without her. I stuck my chin in the air, like Amy did when she was scared or being told off at school, and I said:

'I'm coming to work at the Arsenal, Dad. I'm going to be a munitionette.'

CHAPTER THREE

Dad didn't try to persuade me out of it. He wasn't like that.

'Whatever you decide to do,' he used to say, 'there'll be people who'll tell you not to, say it'll be too hard, you won't like it, it's not for the likes of you. They'll try and stop you, Lily-oh. But you mustn't let them. Listen to me, girl. You Must Not Let Them!'

I always remembered that. So whenever a teacher at school or a man in a shop or an aunty in Silvertown asked me what I wanted to be when I grew up, and I said goalkeeper (like I always did), and they laughed and told me girls couldn't be goalkeepers, dear, not professional ones anyway, it was hard enough for a boy to make his living from playing football, let alone a girl and had I thought about going into service, find a nice position in a big house over the river like their sister's eldest girl, she had a lovely place with ever such a nice family, I'd always say, 'Does she like it then, your sister's eldest? Is she a happy girl?'

And there'd be a pause and then they'd shrug their shoulders and tighten their lips and look away with a sort of sigh and I knew that Mary, or whatever her name was, wasn't a happy girl. That she spent her days on her knees scrubbing someone else's floor and her nights crying herself to sleep in an attic bedroom. And they weren't happy either, the teacher at school, or the man in the shop or the aunty in Silvertown, which is why they said what they did. They didn't want anyone else to be brave or adventurous or different because it would make them feel even worse than they already did about their own lives and all the things they'd never done.

So Dad didn't try to persuade me out of it. He knew I'd made up my mind and that was that.

He was a tall man, my dad, taller than all his mates, and he'd been a goalkeeper in his day, a good one too, for Woolwich Arsenal. He used to take me to see his old team play when I was little, down at the old Manor Ground. I loved it, standing there at the edge of the pitch, eating salted peanuts from a paper bag while the men around us swayed and roared and Dad explained the finer points of the game and sucked air through his teeth every time his team made a mistake. There were a few women there with their husbands and sweethearts, but I was the only little girl and it made me feel special, being there with my dad.

And then Dad lost heart when his team made the move over the river to their new ground at Highbury, way up in north London, and we stopped going.

'It's not the same, Lily-oh,' he said. 'It's all about the money now, it's not for the people of Woolwich, the people that made this town. It's all about money.'

He was right in a way, I suppose. They'd even changed the name. They weren't Woolwich Arsenal any more, just the Arsenal, as if they'd completely forgotten where the team had started. It was like they didn't belong anywhere any more, they didn't have a proper home. I didn't care as much as Dad, though. I quite wanted to see their fancy new ground and I would've made the trip over the river if it wasn't so far.

Dad was the reason I wanted to be a goalkeeper, of course. Every weekend when he wasn't working, we'd be out in the park. We'd make a goal between two little trees and take it in turns to be keeper. Dad always saved the ball when I kicked it, so it was more fun for me to be in goal. I think it was more fun for him too, because he loved to teach me all he knew.

'Watch the player, Lil,' he used to say. 'The player, remember, not the ball.' And I'd try and try, but the ball would fly past. So then he'd say, 'Look at my eyes. My eyes will tell you where I'm going to put the ball.' Sometimes he'd just make me stand there, quite still in my goal, while he shot balls past me again and again and again. 'If you're going to keep goal,' he said. 'You've got to learn to be still and watch.' So I did. 'Control yourself,' he'd say. 'Then, when you know what you're doing, you can move. Otherwise you're just throwing yourself about any old where.'

Once I'd got that, he'd make me shout where I thought the ball was going, still not moving a muscle, just watching his eyes and his body as he struck the ball. 'Left high!' I'd yell. 'Right low!' And when I'd got it right ten times in a row he'd let me try and save it. 'Watch me, Lil,' he'd say. 'Remember. Watch me, not the ball.'

It was hard at first, because he never made it easy for me. I'd concentrate, concentrate, concentrate, watching his eyes, his body, his feet in their heavy old work boots. He'd had proper football boots when he played as a professional all those years ago, but he didn't wear them any more. He kept them in a special box on top of the wardrobe and got them out every Sunday night to oil them. The leather was as soft as silk now, and the boots glowed like fresh conkers. I didn't have any proper football boots myself, of course, so I just wore my everyday ones, even though they were getting a bit tight and my feet would be rubbed raw by the time we went home.

Well, the ball would fly past me again and again and each time I'd run to get it from the middle of a bramble bush or someone's picnic, wherever it had landed, and pick it up, going 'sorry, sorry, sorry', then kick it back to Dad before going back to my place in the goal. 'Not tired yet?' he'd say, never waiting for a reply, and then he'd place the ball for another shot. I was tired, he knew that, but he also knew that I'd not stop until it got too dark to see and the park keeper went round ringing his bell to tell us that he was about to lock the gates for the night.

I missed and I missed and I missed, and my hands stung and my knees throbbed and my feet hurt and the ball still kept flying past me. And then, one day, just as the light was beginning to fade and dark green shadows were stretching out across the grass, it happened.

I've gone through it so many times in my mind since then that it'll be there for ever, scratched into my brain until the day I die. Dad placing the ball, walking back to take his run-up, limping slightly from his bad knee. Me, watching him. He's right-footed, my dad, though he can use his left when he wants. This time I knew he was going to use his right, I don't know how, but I knew. He ran up. His right leg went back and I saw, in that split second, his eyes flick over my left shoulder, and I knew. I knew exactly where the ball was going to go.

BOOF!

Dad's right foot struck the ball and I jumped. I threw myself up, arms outstretched, feeling like I was hanging there in the air for a second, and . . .

I had it. I caught it. I saved my first goal.

Dad was laughing and clapping. He came over to where I'd collapsed in a heap on top of the ball, and picked me up and put me on his shoulders, and we paraded around the park with me holding the ball on his head until the park keeper threw us out, so we went and had an ice cream in the kiosk outside the gates. I don't think I've ever felt so happy in my life.

It felt like a long time ago now, that day in the park when I saved my first goal. Before the war started, before my best friend's brother was killed.

Before I decided to become a munitionette.

CHAPTER FOUR

It was my first day at work and I was so scared I could hardly get out of bed. It was meant to be me and Amy doing this together and now it was just me. I'd had no trouble convincing them about my age at the Labour Exchange. The man filling in the form never even looked up when I told him I was eighteen. He just told me to go along to Number Four Gate at the Arsenal, six-thirty sharp on Monday morning, and report to the lady supervisor in her office.

So I did.

I'd never been inside the Arsenal before, even though I'd lived in its shadow all my life. It was like a huge secret city was hidden behind those great walls, a city that banged and groaned and pumped out evil yellow smoke and coated the whole of Woolwich with its sooty blackness. So when I turned up at the gate and saw all the people streaming in – the girls with their bags, laughing and talking, the men with their heads down – I was so scared I nearly turned right round to go back home. But the policeman at the gate saw me and beckoned me over, then checked my form and showed me where to go.

'Don't worry, love,' he said. 'All the other young girls was just as scared as you on their first day. You'll be fine.' And then he grinned, which made me feel a bit better.

The lady supervisor's office was in a little build-ing just inside the gate, and the lady supervisor was called Miss Barker. She was a big square woman wearing a hat and a sort of uniform, like a man's (but with a skirt instead of trousers, of course). She looked at my form, then sent me through to see a lady doctor who checked me over to make sure I was fit. That was embarrassing, because I had to take off most of my clothes, but she said I passed with flying colours which was good. Then I had to get dressed in my work clothes. There was a sort of brownish overall thing, a bit stiff and oily and much too short in the arms, and a floppy cloth cap to cover my hair. I was sure I looked a complete fright, but luckily there was no mirror so I couldn't tell.

'You'll have to tuck your hair up, dear,' the lady supervisor said. 'You don't want it catching in the machines.' I'd be working in the New Fuse Factory, she went on, helping to make the bombs so our boys could blow up other girls' boys (she didn't say that, of course, but it's what I was thinking), and she told me where to go when I left her office. 'Follow the other girls,' she said. 'And don't take any notice of the men. Some of them don't like women working here. But we're all on the same side, so rise above it if you can, dear, rise above their nonsense.'

I was still scared, but I did what she said. I left the office and joined the stream of girls making their way across a scrubby bit of grass. I don't think I'd ever seen so many girls in one place before. There were women too, some as old as Amy's mum, all in these brownish overalls like mine, but some with trousers underneath. Some had stuck flowers in their caps and threaded ribbons into their boots in place of the dull brown laces, emerald green and scarlet and yellow, and they were walking arm in arm, leaning on each other and laughing, laughing, laughing, all the time. I could see some of them looking at me out of the corners of their eyes, but none of them said anything.

The men stood around silently in doorways watching the girls as they went past, with looks on their faces that I didn't understand, but the girls didn't seem to care. Some younger boys were running around, fooling with the girls and saying stuff that made them laugh and aim little slaps at their heads. The boys ducked and then went straight back for more. I saw Tommy Thompson from school (who I knew for a fact was younger than me), but I didn't want him to see me, so I kept my head down and walked on.

The New Fuse Factory was a long, low building, sooty-black with grime just like all the others. There was another lady at the door, a tall thin one this time, also wearing a hat. I told her who I was and that I was new, and she told me she was the overlooker for my section. I was to call her Miss

Foxwell and come to her if I had any problems, dear, any problems at all. And then we went inside. 'Follow me, dear,' she said. So I did.

It was gloomy inside the workshop, the windows shuttered against the sun, and it took a few moments for my eyes to adjust to the light and make out the shapes around me. It was like a city built of machines, rows and rows and rows, streets and streets of machines, all grinding and clanking and thumping, with girls and women feeding things into them, sorting things out, heaving things around. I couldn't tell what was part of the machine and what was actually being made.

I'm never going to be able to do this, I thought.

I wanted to turn round and run out, but I didn't, because that would've been more embarrassing than carrying on. I often think that embarrassment is the biggest emotion of all, bigger than fear, bigger than sadness even. So I followed Miss Foxwell between the machines, keeping my eyes on the back of her jacket, trying not to look at the girls who were eyeing me as we walked past.

I'm never going to be able to do this, I thought again, but then I heard something. It was just one girl at first, one clear voice ringing out across the workshop, like a single bird above the marshes, singing along with the rhythm of the machines.

'*She's my lady love, she is my dove, my baby love . . .*'

It was my song, the song I used to hear Mum singing around the house in the long summer evenings when I got home from school.

'*She's no girl for sitting down to dream, she's the only queen Laguna knows . . .*'

And as I listened, standing there between the rows of machines, another voice joined in, then another:

'*I know she likes me, I know she likes me, because she says so . . .*'

Until all the girls in the workshop seemed to be singing to me in time with the machines:

'*She is my Lily of Laguna, she is my Lily and my rose . . .*'

And I knew I was going to be all right because the girls were singing my song. It was as if they were welcoming me to their factory.

'What's this?'

A voice cut through my thoughts, interrupting the song. The man was tall, taller than me, and about the same age as Amy's Arthur, but that was the only thing they had in common. Arthur had fair curls and a big broad open face that was always laughing and looking at you as if you were the most interesting thing he'd ever seen. This man had lank black hair that hung over his forehead and a pale, greasy face with spots round his mouth. But it was the look on that face that made my stomach clench. He was leaning against a pillar next to one of the machines and looking at me with such a look as I'd never seen before. It was like I was a black beetle that'd crawled across his naked foot when he was getting into bed, or a maggot in an apple he'd just bitten.

'Ah, Crawford,' said Miss Foxwell. 'This is your new girl.' She didn't seem to notice his expression. She was one of those nice, ladylike women who sees the best in everyone and thinks everyone in the world is basically like her. 'Her name's Lily Dodd,' she went on. 'She's a big strong girl and she's eager to learn. Show her the ropes, will you?'

'Yes, ma'am,' he said. And he touched his forehead with one finger as if he was wearing a cap. My dad would've hated that, would've called him a crawler. 'People have to earn your respect, Lil,' he used to say. 'You don't give it to someone just because they've got a lah-di-dah voice or more money than you. They've got to earn it.'

And then she was gone, the lady overlooker, and I was alone with him. Around us the machines clattered and banged and the girls sang on. He waited until Miss Foxwell was completely out of sight before he turned to look at me again. The sneer had come back to his face, and my legs were shaking.

'That's *Mr* Crawford to you,' he said. '*Dodd*.' He spat out my last name as if it was a piece of rotten meat. 'Follow me.'

I followed him down the aisle between the machines, watching his boots on the greasy black floor and knowing that I'd made the first enemy of my life. I've made others since then, but none who hated me as much as Joe Crawford. I could tell he hated me from that first moment on my very first day.

I just didn't know why.

CHAPTER

FIVE

The work was easy once I got the hang of it, and I got the hang of it quickly in spite of my big goalkeeper's hands. I had a pile of these circular bits of metal – brass, I think, not that it mattered – and I had to grind the rough edges off them on a wheel on my machine. And that was it. I could see Joe Crawford watching me, hoping I'd make a mistake so he could sneer and feel like he was right, girls couldn't do men's work, but to be honest I didn't care. I'd come across boys like him at school, some girls too, actually. Those people who don't like anyone new coming along and being good at anything, and will do everything they can to make you feel bad.

I wondered why Joe Crawford was like that, and

found myself thinking I'd talk to Amy May about it because she was always interested in stuff like that. Then I remembered I wasn't going to see her, not for a long time, and I felt my eyes prickle and the bit of metal I was holding against the grinder nearly jumped out of my hands. I saw Crawford grin to himself, pleased that I'd nearly made a mistake.

The morning passed quickly and then a hooter went off. A little cheer went up from the other girls and they all started clattering around and finishing what they were doing, picking up their things and heading for the door. I supposed it must be dinner time. I'd brought sandwiches in a brown paper bag, like I used to at school. But at school, I could sit and eat them with Amy, in the classroom if it was cold or out in the playground when it was nice, sitting in the sun with our backs against the warm brick wall. But Amy wasn't here. There were just hundreds and hundreds of other girls who all seemed to know each other and all seemed to know exactly what they were doing. I was the only girl who didn't know anybody – and it wasn't like I could hide. When you're five foot ten in your socks it's quite hard to disappear into a crowd.

I didn't know what to do. Was I meant to go too? Perhaps it was just for them and if Crawford or somebody else saw me leave my machine I'd get told off. Or I'd get the sack. I didn't think I could bear that on my first day, so I finished grinding the last of my brass circles and put it on the pile with the others and then just stood there as the other girls walked past, wondering what to do and feeling stupid. And then I heard a voice:

'And this is our latest recruit, Lady Dorothy. A fine strong girl who started today and goes by the name of Lily Dodd.'

It was Miss Foxwell with another lady who was looking up at me with a little smile on her face. She wasn't in a uniform like the other ladies. She was wearing a beautiful jacket – purple, with a matching skirt and a big hat with white ostrich feathers that trembled when she moved.

'How do you do, Lily?' she said. 'Are you enjoying your first day at the Arsenal?' And then she held out her hand. I looked down at it and saw she was wearing gloves. Gloves! On such a hot day to be wearing gloves, white ones that went all the way up under the sleeves of her jacket. It made me think of another hot day, when Amy and I were ten and we'd gone to Brighton on the Sunday School trip. We'd never been to the seaside before and we stood on the beach with the waves slooshing round our legs, gazing, just gazing, at the soft blue line where the sea meets the sky.

'Look, Lil,' Amy said. 'Out there. That's France, that is.'

We stood there for a minute looking at it and then I shouted, '*parley voo!*' because that was the only bit of French I knew, and then Amy said '*ooh la la!*' and we laughed and then, when we'd finished laughing, Amy turned to me with her funny eyes shining and said, 'I'm going to go there one day, Lil. And the first thing I'll do when I get there, I'll go into a fancy French shop and I'll buy a lovely French hat for me and a pair of Dainty White Gloves for my mum.' She said it like that, as if the words had capital letters, like in an advertisement in the newspaper.

I nearly laughed out loud, standing there at my machine in the workshop, thinking about how happy we were.

'Ahem!'

Miss Foxwell coughed and slid her eyes towards the feather-hat lady's outstretched hand. Of course! I was meant to shake it. I'd never shaken anybody's hand before. Amy always gave me a friendly shove when we met, my aunties kissed me and other grown-ups – teachers and so on – would usually just fold their arms and look at me down their noses like I was a bad smell on legs. And Dad never really did anything when I got in from school. He'd just look up from his paper or the boots he'd been cleaning, and beam as if the sight of me was the most beautiful thing in the world.

Now I had to shake the hand of this important-looking lady visitor in the feathery hat with my hands all black and smeary from the machine. But she smiled at me, and Miss Foxwell gave a little nod, so I wiped my right hand on the back of my overall then took her hand and gave a sort of little bobbing curtsey, because I was so much taller than her and I was embarrassed. Then I realized I was supposed to say something. She'd asked me if I was enjoying my first day at the Arsenal.

'I wouldn't say I'm exactly enjoying it, ma'am,' I

said. 'But I shall certainly enjoy my pay packet at the end of the week.'

That must have been the wrong thing to say, because Miss Foxwell gave a little gasp, but the feathered-hat lady's mouth twitched and she patted my arm. 'Good for you, Lily,' she said. 'A miss is as good as a man, eh?'

'Yes, ma'am,' I said, though I had no idea what she meant.

And then Miss Foxwell said, 'Well! Shall we?' and the other lady said, 'Enjoy your lunch, Lily,' and off they went. So that was it. It took a stranger who was being shown round the factory to let me know it was my dinner break. I picked up the paper bag with my sandwiches and headed for the door.

After the gloom of the workshop, the sunshine hit me like a wall. For a moment I was nearly blinded. All I was aware of was light and laughter and vague shapes of people moving around in the glare. And there were shouts:

'Over here!'

'To me!'

'Jess! Jess!'

'Peggy!'

And then:

'Watch it!'

Something was flying through the air towards me. I ducked just in time and it hit the wall behind my head and bounced off. And I saw what it was.

It was a football. They were playing football, only five-a-side, but proper football, a proper game, with goals marked out with their bags and stuff. And they were all girls.

I couldn't believe it. My first day at work as a munitionette at the Royal Arsenal and I was standing there on that scrubby piece of grass, with the dog daisies and the ragwort blowing in the sun, watching girls playing football. They were playing it properly, you see, like boys.

Like me.

I suddenly felt really shy, embarrassed almost, like a dog who's lived among people all their life and is suddenly introduced to other dogs for the first time. I wanted to join in, of course I did. But I would've died rather than ask. So I sat down to eat my sandwiches in a sheltered place by the wall where I could see them but they wouldn't notice me. A handful of men were watching too, pretending they weren't really interested (though I could tell they were), and there were a couple of boys, one retrieving the ball when it went out of play and one playing in goal. There was a girl in goal at the other end, a funny round girl, who kept falling over and laughing every time the ball flew past her. She wasn't very good, but there was one girl, a girl wearing trousers, who had a serious, determined face and dark hair that was all sort of gingery round the front as if it had been burnt. She was as good as any man. Better, even.

So I sat there. I ate my sandwiches. I watched. The time passed. Out of the corner of my eye I saw that Miss Foxwell and the lady visitor in the feathered hat had appeared and were standing together talking and half-watching the girls playing football. Then the hooter sounded for the end of break and Miss Foxwell checked her watch. I got up and brushed the grass off my overalls, the men started to drift back to their workshops and the dark-haired girl took one last almighty kick at the ball, as if she was angry that they had to stop playing. I could see where it was going to go because I was watching her, not the ball. It was heading at about a hundred miles an hour straight for the feathery hat of the lady visitor, where it was bound to do some serious damage, not just to the hat but to the lady's pretty head.

I didn't stop to think. I dropped the screwed-up paper bag my sandwiches had been in and flung myself through the air, drew back my right arm and...

BOFF!

Just in time. I punched the ball away, an instant before it hit her. My knuckles didn't half hurt.

There was a shocked pause.

The lady visitor turned, a bit surprised. She hadn't even realized what a narrow squeak she'd just had. She patted her soft brown hair and smiled at us in a vague way and then Miss Foxwell said again, 'Shall we?' and they moved away.

And that was when I realized that everybody else was looking at me. All the girls who'd been playing football, all the boys and men who were still there, were looking at me, staring. Some of them had their mouths open. One of the boys had picked up the ball from where it had fallen on the grass. None of them said a word.

Then the dark-haired girl, the one whose shot had nearly knocked the feathered hat off the head of the important lady visitor, strode across and slapped me on the back. She grinned and turned to the others. 'Ladies,' she said, 'I think we've found our goalkeeper!'

And as the other girls cheered and clapped and gathered round to pat me on the back and ask me my name, I saw him. Joe Crawford, watching from the darkness of the doorway, with a look on his face that made me feel afraid.

CHAPTER SIX

'**D**ad! Dad-dad-dad! DAD!'

I flew home from the factory that day, my feet never even touched the pavement. And there was Dad sitting at the bottom of the stairs in the little house in Spray Street as always, putting on his boots ready for his night shift. He looked up as I crashed through the front door, a big broad smile on his dear face, but before I could blurt out my news a thought dropped into my head. It seemed to come from nowhere and it stopped me in my tracks.

He looks old, said the thought. *He won't be around for ever.*

I pushed the thought away. Dad wasn't old, I told it. Not compared to someone like Amy's grandma who only had one tooth in her entire mouth, or my Aunty Em who lived across the river in Silvertown and always smelt of cabbage. But Dad had never been the same since Mum died, that's what everyone said, and recently even I'd noticed that he'd changed. He was too old to play for his team, too old for the army. Soon he'd be too old to work at the Arsenal, and then what would happen?

He'd been getting slower too. It was like his legs creaked when he moved. And in the evenings when we were sitting together in the front room after tea, I would look up from my mending to see him staring into the air above his newspaper, looking at nothing. I wasn't worried about him, not *worried*. It was just that he didn't seem very happy any more, and I couldn't bear that. But all that was going to change as soon as he heard my news, I knew it was.

'Well?' Dad said. 'How'd you get on at the Arsenal, Lily-oh? How's my brave munitionette?'

'It was fine, Dad,' I said. 'The work. It was good. Easy. Boring. But DAD!' I stopped. My news was so wonderful that I didn't know how to tell it.

'Dad!' I said again, and again, the words got stuck in my throat.

Dad waited, looking at me with the smile still on his face. He had little triangles of hair on his cheekbones that got left when he shaved, and those small grey bristles made my heart ache.

'What's up, Lil?' he said. 'You look like someone just gave you a hundred pounds.'

'It's better than that, Dad.'

'Two hundred?'

'Better.'

He waited. I waited. It was so quiet that I could hear the tick of the clock from the front room. Mum wasn't singing tonight. She was waiting to hear my news too. Then the words jumped out of my mouth.

'I'm going to be in a team, Dad.'

He stared at me. His mouth was open.

'What?'

'A proper team. Of girls.'

He said nothing, just carried on looking at me. And then the words started to tumble out so fast that there was no stopping them. 'They're called the Arsenal Rockets, Dad, the Rockets, and they're in a proper league and they play proper matches against other girls' teams and, Dad!' I stopped and then laughed because I was so happy. And he laughed too because I was laughing and he knew what I was going to say.

'Dad! I'm going to be in goal!'

Dad didn't go to work that night. He got his mate Stan, who lived next door and kept chickens, to tell them he was poorly, and he gave up a night's pay to sit up with me, dreaming, making plans and talking, talking, talking.

But first, we danced.

Dad swept me up in his arms and we waltzed down the tiny hallway and into the front room, round and round until we were sick and dizzy from spinning and laughing and joy.

'. . . The captain's called Jess, Dad.' I'd collapsed in an upright chair by the window and had just got my breath back. 'She's really something. Her hair's all orange at the front like it's been burnt.'

Dad was in the old armchair by the fireplace. 'Chemicals,' he said, wiping his forehead with a handkerchief. 'Shouldn't be allowed.'

'Yes, she works in the Danger Buildings. In trousers!' Dad grinned at my glee. 'But she's such a player, Dad!' I went on. 'She's got a kick on her like I've never seen. Better than any girl. Better than most boys. Most men!'

'Position?' said Dad.

'Centre-forward.'

'What about the others?'

'There's a girl with a left foot, she was really fast. Polly, I think her name is. And a couple of decent defenders who seem to know what they're doing. But Jess, she's the best. Been playing as long as me, ever since she was little. She's got brothers, you see. One's a pro – or was before he joined up.'

'Arsenal?'

'Spurs.'

'Nobody's perfect.'

We grinned at each other. Arsenal supporters were meant to hate Spurs, and Spurs to hate Arsenal. But we were above all that, me and Dad. We just loved football.

'Anyway, he's in France now, with the Footballers' Battalion.'

'Waste.'

'Yeah, I know, but . . . Dad!' I looked across at him. 'Jess says the team's good, but they could be so much better. They need a manager. And, Dad – I told her about you, and she wants you to do it.'

Dad said nothing, so I carried on.

'Billy Cracken could be your assistant. He's not the best player in the world, but no one knows more about football or loves it more. Dad? Why don't you say something? What d'you think?'

Dad still didn't speak. He got up, unfolding his long body slowly and carefully from the chair. He had an old injury from his playing days, and his left knee still gave him gyp sometimes.

'Dad?'

He didn't say a word, just turned walked out of the room. I listened to his footsteps thudding up the stairs and felt my heart beating all over my body. Mum was looking down at me. *It'll be fine*, her eyes said. *You know what he's like, Lily. Only opens his mouth if he's got something to say.*

I felt her fingers stir in my hair and smelt her familiar scent of dust and violets. Dad's footsteps were coming back down. The door opened and he came in, lowering his head to get through the doorway.

'These are for you,' he said.

What?

He was holding his boots.

'*What?*'

The boots that he'd saved for week after week when he'd got his first job at the Arsenal as a boy, putting the pennies into a jar on the mantelpiece after he'd handed over the shillings to his mum. The boots that had played every game with him when he got his place in the team, that he'd never replaced even when he was getting paid to play games on a Sunday on top of his normal wage, because by then the boots were lucky and he was scared to get a new pair in case his luck ran out. The boots he still oiled every Sunday night even thought he'd played his last game in them over fourteen years ago, before I was born.

'I want you to have them, Lil.'

I didn't know what to say, so I said, 'Will they fit?'

'Let's see.'

His bad knee cracked as he knelt down on the rug at my feet. I kicked off my right boot and stretched out my foot. My big toe was sticking out of the stocking but I didn't care. Dad looked up at me and grinned. I could tell he wanted to make a joke about smelly feet (and I expect they were smelly after my day in that hot workshop) but we both knew that this moment was far too serious for jokes. He loosened the laces in the right football boot and held it out to me like a man in a shoe shop. The leather gleamed, soft and supple with the loving care Dad had lavished on it for all those years. I slipped my foot inside, like Cinderella.

'It fits, Dad,' I said. 'It fits.'

CHAPTER SEVEN

'Lily Dodd! Are you listening to me?'

I'd been working at the Arsenal for a month now and was sitting with Jess at a long table in the women's canteen, eating my sandwiches and watching the sparrows flying in and out through the open door. The room smelt of girls and sunshine and cabbage, and an old lady in a hat was banging out tunes on a piano in the corner. 'You've got a treat today, girls,' Miss Foxwell had announced that morning. 'An important lady visitor! The Duchess of Richmond is coming to play for you!' It wasn't much of a treat, to be honest. The piano was out of tune, and the Duchess's playing wasn't up to much.

'I wonder if they wear their hats in the bath,' I

said. 'These Important Lady Visitors. What do you reckon, Jess?' It was the sort of question Amy May loved. She and I would've talked about it for hours, doing funny voices and laughing till our stomachs hurt. I'd only had one postcard from her since she'd gone, with a couple of lines of her mad loopy writing telling me she was leaving for France and that she'd write soon. Since then, nothing.

'You haven't heard a word I've said, have you?' Jess was shovelling down her usual sausage and mash and talking with her mouth full. She wasn't interested in the kind of daft things Amy and I liked to talk about. 'We've got a friendly next Sunday, so we need to get started on some proper training. When's your dad free?'

'He's working nights at the moment,' I said. 'So it'll have to be Sunday.'

One of the sparrows had landed on top of the piano and was sitting there with his head on one side, giving the Duchess a beady look.

'Sunday it is.' Jess scraped up the last bit of mash from her plate and licked her knife on both sides. Then she got a little notebook out of the pocket of her overall and took a pencil stub from behind her ear. 'We're not allowed to use the Manor Ground for training, just games, so where will it be? Woolwich Common?'

'Hello, Jess.'

A fair-haired girl sat down at our table. She was pretty in what my Aunty Em called a 'lah-di-dah' way, with round blue eyes and yellow curls arranged carefully round her face. Her smile was small and sharp like the scratch of a pin.

'Who's your new friend?' Her eyes flicked over me rapidly before she looked away. It was clear she wasn't impressed with what she saw.

'Her name's Lily,' said Jess without looking up.

'What a sweet name! How do you do, Lily.'

She held one limp hand out to me across the table. I was embarrassed by my big sweaty paw, and wiped it secretly on my overall before I took her hand. 'Pleased to meet you,' I said.

This was a lie. I wasn't pleased to meet her at all. If I'm honest, which I usually am, I didn't really like the look of her. I don't often tell lies, but I didn't know what else to say. Amy May used to tell lies all the time and not just because she didn't know what else to say or to get out of trouble. She sometimes just did it for fun. She once told a new teacher at school that she was the long-lost daughter of the Duke of Plumstead and that she had a terrible fear of owls.

'Jess has no manners.' The girl leant confidentially across the table to me. 'She spends so much time thinking about football she has no idea how to behave in polite company.'

'What do you want, Dora?' Jess spoke without looking up.

Dora put her head on one side and smiled at nothing. 'I'm collecting little notes and tokens for the boys,' she said.

Jess rolled her eyes, but I was interested.

Dora leant across to me again. 'I'm sending some of my latest photographs,' she said. 'Would you like to see, Lily? I've just picked them up.'

Without waiting for a reply she reached into the green cloth bag she had over her arm and pulled out a photograph. It was tiny, about as big as one of the dry biscuits Amy's mum used to give us with our milk when I went round to their house after school.

'It's you!' I said, looking at Dora. 'Isn't it?'

The girl in the picture had her head on one side and a silly sort of smile on her face. She was sitting on a farm gate in front of a painted backdrop of trees and sky, dressed up in a sort of milkmaid's outfit, all frills and ribbons, with a bunch of dead-looking flowers hanging from one hand. Jess had a quick look over my shoulder and snorted, then went back to her notebook.

'You look very pretty,' I said.

Dora looked down and smiled at her nails. I wondered how she kept them so clean.

'What's it for?' I went on. 'Where did you say you're sending them?'

'They write notes to the soldiers,' said Jess. 'Out at the front.'

'Oh?'

'To remind them of home, poor dears,' said Dora. 'With pressed flowers or photographs or sweeties, any little tokens we can think of. And then we tuck them in amongst the shells and bullets before they get sent over to France.'

I was interested. 'So, what, the men find them when they're unpacking the munitions?'

'That's right.' There was that smile again. 'Don't

you think it's a lovely idea, Lily?'

Jess sniffed. 'I'm sure it makes the boys feel a whole lot better about being shot at by Germans,' she said.

'Any little thing we can do to lighten their load.' Dora folded her lips together. 'The poor boys, they don't have much to look forward to.'

'And a picture of you dressed up as a milkmaid will make all the difference,' said Jess.

Dora tossed her head. 'I think it's the least we can do,' she said. 'And besides –' she gave me a sideways look from under her eyelashes – 'some of the girls have got letters back, Lily! One even had a proposal of marriage!'

'Really?' It seemed unbelievable that a man would want to marry a girl he'd never met. 'So she's a married woman now?'

'Oh no, I'm afraid not.' Dora looked past me, out of the open door of the canteen at the sunshine beyond and bit her lip. She had small, square teeth like a baby's. 'I'm sorry to say, Lily, that he . . . he never came home.' She gave a long shuddery sigh and looked down at her hands as if to hide her tears.

I felt terrible. 'Oh. I'm sorry,' I said. 'I didn't mean . . .'

Dora gave herself a little shake and tucked her photograph away in her bag. 'But still!' she said, perfectly cheery again. 'I'm sure her letters brought some sunshine to his last days!'

Jess rolled her eyes. 'I'm sure they did, Dora. Now if you don't mind, we're busy.'

'Oh, you and your football!' Dora stood up. 'You'll never get a sweetheart like that, Jess Jones! The boys don't like it, you know. Girls acting like men, running around getting all dirty and hot. Showing their knees! It's not what I call ladylike.'

I watched her as she walked off between the tables, swinging her bag in time with the music, and thought about what she'd said. It sounded fun, to write a note and put it somewhere for a soldier to find.

'Who was that girl, Jess?' I said.

'Her name's Dora Crawford.'

'Crawford?' The sound of the out-of-tune piano and the girls' chatter suddenly seemed to be coming from a long way away.

'I was at school with her,' Jess went on. 'She's a

right piece of work. Never thinks of nothing but looking pretty and flirting with boys.' She sniffed and flicked a bit of spilt mashed potato at a sparrow perched on the end of our table. He fixed it with one beady eye, then gave it a quick jerky peck as if he hoped nobody would notice.

'Did you say her name was Crawford?'

'What? Yeah. Dora Crawford. She works in the tailor's shop, sewing gas masks and overalls and stuff. No chance of her hair turning yellow and her teeth falling out.' Jess pulled at the bits of burnt-looking hair sticking out from under her cap and squinted up at them.

'Jess? It doesn't really make your teeth . . . ?'

Jess shrugged. 'Oh, I don't know, just makes you go a bit yellow after a while.' She spread out her hands and looked at her nails. For the first time I saw they were yellow too and that her skin had a faint yellowish tinge. 'Drinking milk makes it go away. But that Dora Crawford! Ugh. Thinks she's better than everybody else because her dad's got a shop and her brother used to be a pro.'

'He was a footballer?'

Jess looked at me from under her eyebrows.

'Goalkeeper.'

'Goalkeeper?'

'Yup.' She flicked another speck of potato at the sparrow. 'Joe Crawford. Played for the Arsenal up at Highbury till they stopped the men's game. A lot of players joined the Footballers' Battalion and went off to fight, but not him, oh no. He wasn't about to put his life on the line for his country. Got a nice job in munitions to keep himself out of it.'

'What's he like as a keeper?'

Jess shrugged. 'Never saw him play. But I heard he was all right. Good, even.'

For a second we both watched the sparrow peck at the mashed potato, jerking like a little clock-work toy.

'He works here, doesn't he?' I said.

Jess looked at me. 'How d'you know that?'

'He's the overseer of my section. He hates me.'

'I wouldn't worry about it. Joe Crawford hates everybody, girls particularly. He's just like that, always has been. Nasty. He wanted to manage the Rockets, but I wasn't having it. I could tell he just fancied the idea of throwing his weight about with a group of girls and making us doubt ourselves. There's something about girls playing football that really gets under his skin. He hates all of us.'

'No, but he *really* hates me, Jess. And I don't know why.'

Jess rolled her eyes. 'Well, if you can't work it out, Lily Dodd, you're not as bright as I thought you were.'

'I'm not, then. Because I don't. Tell me.'

Jess sighed and put her notebook away. 'You're a goalkeeper,' she said. 'You're better than him – he saw that on your first day here. You're a girl. And . . . you've got lovely hair.' She counted each statement out on her fingers, then got up quickly, as if she was angry, and picked up her plate.

I couldn't believe my ears. 'What?' I said, as she turned to go. 'Jess? Wait!'

She stopped without turning round, her back looking stiff and annoyed. Then, she swung round to look at me. Her fork fell off the plate and landed on the floor with a clatter.

'What?' She flung the word at me like a cricket ball.

'Have I really got lovely hair?'

Jess gave me a long level look. Then she shook her head, turned and walked on without stopping to pick up the fork, dumped her plate at the serving hatch, and made her way over to the door. After she'd gone I sat there, alone at the long table, with the clatter and chatter of the girls and the smell of sweat and gravy all around me. I stared at the crumbs on the table and traced a smiling face next to them in spilt tea.

I had lovely hair!

That night when I got home and Dad had gone to work and I'd eaten the last bit of cold pie for my tea, I found an old writing pad and a pencil and sat down at the kitchen table. I sucked the end of the pencil for a bit, and then began.

Dear Soldier, (I wrote in my most careful handwriting), *I hope this finds you in the pink. My name is Lily Dodd and I have just started work at the Royal Arsenal in Woolwich. I live with my father in Woolwich. His name is Bob Dodd. He also works at the Arsenal. My mother is dead. Her name was Violet Dodd. If you would like to I would like it if you wrote back to me but only if you would like to. I have put my address at the top of this note. The weather here in Woolwich is sunny. Is it sunny in France? Well that's all for now so I'll say cheerio.*

From

Lily Dodd (aged 17 yrs)

I worried a bit about telling a lie to a soldier, but reckoned if he knew I was only fourteen he might not want to write back. I folded the note carefully, put it in an envelope and wrote *TO A SOLDIER* on the front. The next day I found Dora Crawford at dinner time and asked her to put it with the others in the next case of shells that was going to the front.

And then I forgot all about it.

PART TWO
Autumn 1917

CHAPTER EIGHT

'**O**i! Lil!'

It was Peggy, the Rockets' left-back, calling from the door of the canteen. She was a bit older than the other girls (they were all older than me, of course, but I wasn't going to tell them that) and she'd worked in the Danger Buildings for so long that her face was almost completely yellow and her hair was all brassy-looking as if it had been dipped in something. Even the whites of her eyes had a yellowish tinge. Luckily, whatever it was that had stained her skin and hair didn't seem to affect her game. She was a good player, strong, brave and reliable. Not as good as Jess, of course, but then nobody was that good.

'Lily of Laguna!' she yelled. 'We're waiting

for you!'

I'd been working at the Arsenal for nearly three months now. The work was still boring, Joe Crawford was still nasty, and I hadn't heard from Amy since the postcard saying she was going to France. I missed her, of course I did, and worried about her and wondered what she was doing and if she'd ever get round to writing again, but if I'm honest (which, as I said, I usually am) I didn't think about it all that much. Amy was my best friend and nothing would ever change that, but now I had the Rockets. I was in a team and I had lots of new friends. We hadn't played a match yet, but we trained on the common every Sunday and played every dinner time at work. The bosses had let us paint two white lines on the wall of the workshop for goal posts, and more and more people would come and watch us play: the Canary Girls, who worked with Jess and Peggy in the Danger Buildings, with their yellowish skin and burnt-looking hair, as well as lots of older women and men and boys from all over the factory. Even Miss Barker, the lady supervisor I'd met on my first day, would usually make the effort to come over from her office to watch. I was happy.

Billy Cracken had got a job at Woolwich Barracks looking after the horses, so he was happy too. He still lived in the children's home, but now he came to the common every Sunday to help Dad with training, and then back with us to Spray Street afterwards so we could all eat fish and chips and talk about the Rockets until it got dark.

'LILY!'

'Sorry, sorry, sorry!'

I swallowed down the last of my sandwich, gulped my tea, and ran out to join the game. It was as I was taking my place in the goal that I saw him. He was standing by the workshop door with some other men I hadn't seen before. They were smoking and laughing together, but all the time watching us out of the corners of their eyes while pretending they weren't.

It was Joe Crawford.

He'd never been out there, not since that first day, never been among the people who hung about to watch us during the dinner break, even though we played right outside the New Fuse Factory where he worked. He thought he was too good for

73

it, I suppose, too high and mighty to watch a bunch of girls running around after a ball. So what was he doing there now? He had to be up to something.

'Lily!'

Peggy's voice cut across my thoughts. Jess had got past her and was only a few feet away from my goal. We played five-a-side most days, and Jess and I were always on opposite teams so we could be up against each other.

WHOOSH!

I looked round just in time to see the ball fly past my head and crash against the wall behind me. Joe Crawford smirked. He leant over and said something to one of the other men which made them both laugh and look back at me with grins on their faces. I felt rage rise up in my throat, and for a second was scared I was going to be sick.

Peggy shook her head at me. 'Not like you, Lil,' she said. 'Off with the fairies?'

'I know,' I said. 'I'm sorry.' I picked up the ball and booted it up to our forwards. 'It won't happen again, Peg, I promise.'

But I still couldn't concentrate, watching Crawford and wondering what he was up to, so Jess was able to send ball after ball flying past me until the hooter went for the end of the dinner break. Jess picked up the ball, but I was still watching Crawford as he turned and came swaggering over to us, hands in his pockets, grinning over his shoulder at the other men. He took his cigarette out of his mouth and spat on the ground, then stared at Jess.

'You're not bad for a girl,' he said, looking her up and down as if she was something in a shop he was thinking about buying. I felt my face go very still.

Jess didn't say anything. Crawford looked over his shoulder and grinned at the other men again.

'You might be able to get a ball past another female,' he said, indicating me with a jerk of his head. 'But you'd never get a ball past me.'

Jess stuck her chin in the air and glared back up at him. 'That sounds like a challenge,' she said.

Crawford spat on the ground again. 'Does it?'

'Yes,' said Jess. 'And I accept.'

Word spread fast that the captain of the ladies' football team had taken up a challenge to get a shot past the great Joe Crawford. It seemed like everyone in the factory was talking about it.

'He was a professional, wasn't he?'

'That's right. Kept goal for the Arsenal before the war. Up at Highbury.'

'And she thinks she'll get a goal past him! Tuh!'

When the day arrived so many people came to watch that there was barely room to play. I spotted Dora Crawford, standing with a couple of other girls from the tailor's shop, looking like they had a bad smell beneath their noses, and some men in bowler hats and smart overcoats that I'd never seen before. Miss Barker was there, of course. She'd made the trip across from her office and was standing at the side talking to Miss Foxwell and another important Lady Visitor In A Hat.

I felt my heart pounding as Joe Crawford took his place in my goal. One of the older men was acting as referee (probably because he had his own whistle) and he showed Jess where to place her ball, a few yards in front of the goal. Her face was still and looked white beneath its yellow tinge. She put her ball down on its spot very carefully, as if it was made of glass, then walked back slowly to take her run-up.

Crawford was grinning at the men, bouncing from foot to foot and slapping his hands together. I was standing to the left of the goal, watching Jess. *Watch the player.* As Dad always said, *don't watch the ball, Lily-oh. Watch the player.*

I watched her.

The referee blew his whistle. Jess looked down at the ball. She looked across at Crawford. Then she drew a deep breath, ran her few steps, dropped her left shoulder, drew back her right foot and –

BOOF!

I'd never seen a shot like it. Not from any girl, any man, any player. Never.

And then –

SMACK!

Crawford made a sound that was half-scream and half-yell. The ball had hit his shoulder with a sickening crunch, slamming him up against the wall of the workshop behind him. The ball bounced back to Jess, who calmly tapped it past him into the goal.

There was a heartbeat's pause. Then the referee blew his whistle and ran over to Crawford, who had slithered down the wall and was lying groaning and writing about on the ground, and the girls went mad. They cheered and shouted and bounced and hugged each other and gathered round Jess to pat her on the back and hug and kiss her in a great explosion of joy. Even Miss Barker and the other ladies smiled and went over to shake her hand.

But Jess just stood there, her ball under her arm, looking at Crawford, and so did I. We both knew what had happened. Jess had won the challenge.

But she'd broken Joe Crawford's arm.

CHAPTER NINE

It was a week after the day Jess broke Joe Crawford's arm. I got home from work to find Dad sitting on the stairs as usual, putting on his boots, ready for the night shift. We grinned at each other, as usual, and he said, 'No peace for the wicked,' or something like that, and I said, 'Any of that cold pie left from last night?' and he said, 'Not sure, you might have to go out for fish and chips,' and I said, 'Right you are, Dad, see you in the morning,' and it was all very 'as usual' until Dad reached the front door, when he turned and said, 'Oh, nearly forgot. Letter came for you. Official-looking. From France.'

'France?' My heart flipped. *Amy*, I thought. It had to be from Amy.

'It's on the piano,' said Dad, and then he winked and was gone. The door slammed behind him.

I hurried through to the front room, wondering what the letter could be, hoping it was from Amy, and there it was, propped up on the piano under Mum's picture, an official-looking envelope with my name and address on it.

Miss Lily Dodd

Miss! I thought. Nobody had ever called me that before.

27 Spray Street
Woolwich
London
Angleterre

That was French for 'England', I knew that much from school. And it certainly wasn't Amy's handwriting. She wrote in big sprawling curly letters that seemed to tumble all over the page and try and escape from the edges. Miss Hogweed used to say she was the only girl she knew who could smudge pencil. The writing on this envelope was quite neat, written with a fountain pen. Who could it be from?

I picked up the envelope and held it up to my face to smell it, trying to prolong the moment before I opened it, I don't know why. There were a few dirty fingerprints on it, but it didn't smell of anything, just paper. I held it up to the light, but the envelope was too thick to see what was inside. I couldn't delay any longer.

I opened it.

There was the letter, folded in half, and a small photograph, printed on card. On the back was the name of the photographer's studio where it had been taken, written in gold curly writing, some-where in France, I thought.

I turned it over.

And found myself gazing into a pair of dark eyes that looked at me from beneath a mop of curls. I'd seen photographs that people's brothers had sent them from France or had printed before they left (in case they didn't come back, I suppose) and they were always in uniform, trying to look serious and grown up and not-a-bit-scared. This boy wasn't doing any of that. He was looking out of the picture at me as if I'd just said the funniest thing in the world and at any moment he was going to explode in a shout of delighted laughter. And he wasn't in uniform. He was wearing a football jersey and he had a football under his arm.

He was a footballer.

My fingers were shaking (stupid!) as I pulled the letter out of the envelope. I unfolded it carefully and started to read.

Dear Lily Dodd

Well! What a fight we had over your note! I had to threaten my mate Harry with violence because he reckoned he spotted it first. But I said, no, this one's got my name on it, Harry, so hands off! You know how they say there's a bullet with your name on it? Well, it was like that. When I saw that little envelope sticking out of that case, I knew, I just knew it was meant for me.

So what IS my name, I hear you asking. Well, Lily Dodd, I'll tell you. My name is Jack. Jack Darling. But you can call me Jack. Or Darling, when we get to know each other better . . .

Oof!

I had to stop reading when I got to that bit. This

boy, this wonderful boy, had said I could call him 'Darling'! I know he was joking, but even so. I put the letter down on the top of the piano and went over to look out of the front window. Spray Street looked the same as it always did. Dirty. Grey. A couple of little boys were running around, hiding in passageways and pretending to shoot each other, and two women, both with babies on their hips, were standing in a doorway chatting. A sparrow was pecking at something in the gutter and a cat glared at me from a windowsill across the road. None of them knew I'd got a letter from the most wonderful boy, a boy who was a footballer and who said I could call him darling.

I turned away from the window and went back to my letter.

If you've looked at my photograph, Lily Dodd, which I hope you have because I'm pleased as punch with it (though I'm much better-looking in real life! Swank!), you might have guessed something about me, which is that I'm a bit of a footballer. Used to be with Spurs (you'll have heard of them, coming from

Woolwich as you do, or if you haven't, ask your dad,
or your brother if you've got one!) until I gave it up to
do my bit and joined the 17th Middlesex.

The 17th Middlesex. That was the footballers'
battalion. One of Jess's brothers was with them. The
battalion was formed when they stopped the
men's game after the war started, and it wasn't just
for footballers. Anyone could join – men who
worked at the football clubs, trainers, managers,
even the men who followed the teams. I expect a
lot of them liked the idea of fighting alongside
their heroes.

But Jack Darling wasn't one of them. He was
one of the heroes, a proper footballer, a professional like Jess's brother. Like my Dad.

I read on.

So now I've swapped my football kit for khaki
and I'm over here fighting for King and Country.
Bad luck! But not bad luck that I found your note.
I've got a feeling about this, Miss Lily Dodd, a good
feeling. Will you write to me again now you've seen
my ugly mug?

Ugly? I thought, looking at the little photograph. *You're the handsomest boy I've ever seen!*

I hope you will write, Lily. And if you do, will you send me a photograph back? Please?
All the best for now
Jack Darling

PS I'm 17 too but don't tell anyone. I told them I was 19 so I could enlist and they fell for it. Ha!

PPS Weather here is DAMP! But are we downhearted? NO!

Please write, Lily
From
Jack

I folded the letter up carefully, then looked at the photograph one last time and put them both back in the envelope. Outside the women must have finished their chat and gone indoors, and there was no sign of the boys or the cat. The street was deserted except for an old man smoking in a doorway and a scruffy-looking dog rootling around in some rubbish. And as I looked, the sun came out and the dirty grey street suddenly sparkled with colour. A young woman with a red rose pinned to her jacket appeared from around the corner, walking so fast and so cheerfully that she was almost skipping. She grinned at the old man as she passed, and he took his cigarette out of his mouth and raised his cap to her.

I turned back to the room. There was a mirror above the fireplace that had come from Mum's family. It was quite a fancy one, with a gold frame, but old and misty and spotted. It made you feel like you were looking at yourself through a fog. I didn't mind that actually.

I'm not a pretty girl, I know that. I'm too tall, too lanky, too all-over big. My shoulders are too wide, my chest's too flat, my hands are like shovels, my hair's too red and too wiry and there's much too much of it. If Jack saw what I looked like, he'd never want to write to me again, and I didn't think I could bear that. So I wasn't going to send a photograph even if I had one, which I hadn't. And I couldn't tell him what I was really like either, that I probably loved football as much as he did. I thought about what Dora Crawford had said.

'*The boys don't like it, you know. Girls acting like men, running around getting all dirty and hot. Showing their knees! It's not what I call ladylike.*'

I didn't hold much store by Dora Crawford or her opinions, but on this I reckoned she was right. I could tell by the looks on the faces of a lot of the men who watched us play at dinner time. They seemed fascinated and disgusted at the same time, like they'd just been introduced to some new and particularly horrible sort of caterpillar. There was fear in there too. Yes, they looked afraid. I don't know why.

I made up my mind there and then that I wouldn't let on to Jack that I loved football, and I certainly wouldn't let him know that I played. The girl Jack Darling would want to write to, I decided, wouldn't be someone like me, a not-pretty girl, five feet ten in her socks with feet so big they fit into her dad's football boots. It would be someone like Amy. Little and sweet, with curling fair hair and a nose that wrinkled up when she laughed.

So I decided I'd be her.

I went through to the kitchen, got my writing

pad and pencil out from their place behind the clock, and sat down at the table to write.

Dear Jack Darling (I wrote)
I had clean forgot about the note I put in the box of munitions, so I was quite surprised when I found your letter waiting for me at home today—

No, best not put 'today'. Don't want him to think I'm too keen. I tore off the page and started again.

Dear Jack,
I was quite surprised when I got home from work last week to find—

I stopped again. Someone was banging on the door.

'Lily! Lil!' It was Jess, shouting through the letter box. 'Hoy! Lily Dodd! You in there?' She clattered the letter box and carried on thumping the door with her fist as I made my way down the hallway.

'I'm coming! Coming!'

When I opened the door she practically knocked me over in her rush to get inside and share her news. 'It's Crawford,' she said. Her face was flushed and there were beads of sweat on her forehead.

'What about him? Still angry about his arm?'

'It's not that, Lil. He's got himself a team.'

'What?'

'A ladies' team. To manage. The Lyons' Corner House Ladies.'

'What, the Nippies?' That's what people called the waitresses who worked in the Lyons' tea shops all over London, so that was the nickname for the team. They were one of the first ladies' teams in London, had been playing since the early days when the men's game was stopped. 'I've heard they're really good, got their own training ground and everything.'

Jess clutched my arm so hard it hurt. 'Crawford's challenged us to a game,' she said.

'Us? Against the Nippies? Jess! What did you say?'

Jess grinned. 'I said yes,' she said.

Of course she did.

CHAPTER

TEN

The day of the match dawned bright and cold. It was the kind of morning when the whole of London seems to glitter in the sun, when dogs and children run about wildly in parks for no reason and dead leaves swirl in corners on pavements. I'd been woken up by the sound of Billy Cracken hammering at the front door, and I'd lain there for a moment looking at the sunlight on the ceiling and wondering why I felt so scared.

And then I remembered.

Miss Barker had arranged for the match to be played at the old Manor Ground, so, after Dad had told me I really ought to eat a bit of breakfast and Billy tried to distract me by talking about the new horse they had at the barracks (she was a beautiful chestnut mare, with a flash on her nose and four white socks), the three of us set out to walk across the marshes. As we made our way along the river-bank, with the boats calling to each other through the mist and the frosty grass crunching under our feet, I thought back to that hot summer afternoon when Amy and I had lain there, staring at the sky and talking about what we were going to do with our lives. I wished she could be here with me today. Not that she was interested in football, but it would've made her laugh to see us girls running around in the mud with our knees showing, and that would've made me feel less scared.

'Not had any more news of Amy, have you?' Dad always knew what I was thinking.

I shook my head. 'Not since that first postcard.'

Dad nodded. 'Not much of a one for letter-writing, I'm guessing, our Amy May.'

'She'll write again when she's got time,' said Billy.

'Or when she wants something,' I said.

Billy laughed, showing the gap between his front teeth. 'Yes, that's about right. When she wants you to send her some chocolate or food.'

'Or "bars of scented soap",' I said, in the la-di-dah voice Amy and I did to make each other laugh.

'That's right,' said Dad. 'Seriously though, Lil,' he went on, 'you don't need to worry about Amy May. Friends like that never go away.'

'Yeah,' I said and took his hand. 'Yeah, Dad. I know.'

We walked on in silence for a bit, leaving the marshes behind us and turning into the street that bordered the Manor Ground. Dad stopped by a door in the wall that was labelled 'Players' Entrance'.

Players' Entrance.

'This is it, Lily-oh,' said Dad. 'After you.' And he did a funny little bow to show that I should go first.

Billy nodded and gave me a wink which made me feel a tiny bit braver, so I swallowed, opened the door and went through.

'There's so many people.'

Jess was looking out of the changing-room window as the rest of us sat around on the benches, fiddling with our shin pads and lacing up our boots. 'And they're still coming. We're going to have as big a crowd as the men ever did, girls – perhaps even bigger.'

It was obvious that all the other girls were just as nervous as me. We hadn't expected many people to turn up – just friends and family, a couple of Jess's brothers who weren't overseas and some of the girls from work. But then Miss Barker had put the word out about the game, announcing it as a charity match, and had got posters put up all over the factory and on the streets of Woolwich and Plumstead:

LYONS' CORNER HOUSE LADIES V WOOLWICH ARSENAL LADIES

GRAND CHARITY FOOTBALL MATCH TO RAISE MONEY FOR
WOUNDED SERVICEMEN AND THEIR FAMILIES

THE NIPPIES V THE ROCKETS!
COME AND WATCH THE LADIES FIGHT IT OUT!

'I wish Miss Barker had never put up them posters.' This was Polly, inside-right, fast on the ball but tended to lose her nerve in front of the goal. 'I don't think I can play with loads of people staring at me.'

'Nor me.' That was Elsie, centre-half. She was only sixteen but was engaged to be married to a sailor. 'It's embarrassing. All them men looking at our legs, I don't think my Sid would like it.' She stretched out her legs in their striped red-and-white socks and examined them, turning them this way and that. 'I've never thought about my knees before. Never had to, I suppose. Do you think they look normal?'

A couple of the others looked across, and one girl even got up to have a closer look at Elsie's knees.

'I think so. Why?'

'I feel like they're a bit too low down on my legs.'

'If they were any higher up you'd be all unbalanced, Else.'

'Yeah, they look all right to me. Mine are all knobbly.'

'Yours are? Look at mine!'

Soon, nearly all the girls in the team were comparing knees. I could see Jess getting impatient.

'I don't believe you lot,' said Jess. 'We're just about to play our first ever proper match and you're worried about your knees!'

This made everyone laugh. But then Bella spoke up. 'The Nippies are famous, though, aren't they, Jess?' She was studying her face in the mottled mirror on the wall, tucking her hair up into her cap. 'People will have come to see them, not us. Alice! Don't kick the wall like that, you'll damage the paintwork!' Bella always brought her sister along to training to give her mum a break, so we'd made the little girl our mascot. She was sitting on the bench, swinging her legs and watching us all with big eyes. Miss Barker had got the factory bosses to shell out for some kit for us and Alice had a baby version, with dear little shorts and a tiny red-and-white striped jersey.

'They're good too,' said Peggy. 'Best ladies' team in London, my dad says.'

'And we've got them for our first game. Typical.'

'With Joe Crawford in charge.'

'Typical!'

'We're going to lose, aren't we?'

Jess looked up from lacing her boots. 'Button it, Polly. "Course we're not.'

'I don't care about losing,' said Peggy. 'I just don't want to be embarrassed in front of my brother. He says girls can't play football and he's only come to laugh at us.'

'Hoy!' Jess stood up. 'I don't want to hear any more talk of losing, you hear?'

The room went quiet. Jess walked between the benches, her boots crunching on the dried mud on the floor. I picked at a bit of peeling paint with my fingernail and the other girls shuffled uncomfortably on the benches.

'We came here to win,' said Jess. 'And we can win. Look at yourselves, girls. We're strong, we're fast, we've been training hard . . . we're munitionettes, for goodness' sake. I think we can beat a bunch of waitresses!'

That made us laugh again.

'They might be "nippy",' said Jess. I wondered if she'd prepared this speech in advance. It would be like her to do something like that, she took her role as captain that seriously. 'But we,' she went on, 'are the Rockets!' She jumped on to one of the benches and yelled, 'Who are we, girls?'

'The Rockets!' a few of us replied, feeling a bit silly.

'I can't hear you! Who are we?'

'The Rockets!'

'Who are we?'

'You're the Rockets.' Dad stuck his head round the door and looked at the clock on the wall. 'It's time, ladies,' he said.

Jess jumped off the bench and the rest of us got up slowly, checking boots and shin pads and fiddling with our hair. My legs were shaking.

'Right, then,' said Jess. 'Let's get out there and have some fun.'

We lined up – Jess at the front, holding Alice's hand, and me at the back, feeling very tall and embarrassed – and walked out on to the pitch. Going from the dingy little corridor, with its peeling paint and its smell of old sandwiches and damp and football boots, was like stepping into another world. The daylight and the roar of the crowd hit us like a wall. The pitch was laid out at our feet, a huge, muddy-green carpet, walled in on four sides by people, like some great outdoor room. And there were so many people. Both stands were full, and there were more, men and boys mostly, lined up shoulder to shoulder along the touchlines. I couldn't believe it. All these people had come to see us play. Us!

I could see Joe Crawford standing at the side, smoking and smirking, and a white-faced Billy, next to Dad. Dad held out his hand to little Alice, who ran over to him, looking like she was glad to get away from us, and Bill's face cracked into a grin. The Nippies were out on the pitch already. They looked confident and pretty in their black-and-white kit, bouncing about on their feet and smiling and waving to the crowd. One of them was even blowing kisses.

'I can't do it, Lil,' whispered Polly as we walked out, the crowd roaring around us like some huge animal. 'I can't play with all these people watching. I feel sick.'

'Shut up,' I hissed, though I was feeling pretty sick myself. 'You're here now. You've got to.'

'I can't.' She was nearly in tears. 'Listen to them, Lil. They're laughing at us.'

She was right. A lot of the men and boys were laughing and shouting rude comments.

'What's the weather like up there?' a bloke at the front yelled at me. 'Lanky legs!'

That did it. I felt the familiar flare of anger rise up in my chest and burn my cheeks. I turned to Polly. 'Then we'll just have to show them, won't we? We'll soon wipe the silly smiles off their faces.'

The referee beckoned the two captains over and tossed a coin. Jess won. That meant she chose which end to play and the others kicked off. She pointed to the south end of the pitch, so the wind was behind us for the first half. Good. We all ran to our positions. I took my place in my goal. Alone, but part of the team. I didn't feel nervous any more. I was ready.

The whistle blew. The crowd roared. The game was on.

For a moment the Rockets just stood there, stunned and frozen. But the Nippies had done this before. Their forwards fell on the ball and were heading towards my goal before my teammates realized what was happening. Jess was the first to wake up.

'Defence!' she shouted. 'Get on them!'

She came charging down to support, but the Nippies' forwards were already past our half-backs.

'Away!' I yelled. 'Away!'

Peggy made a half-hearted move to tackle the player with the ball, but she fluffed it and fell over in the mud.

'Up!' I shouted. 'Peggy! Get up!'

My other full-back moved over to help, but instead of trying to tackle the girl with the ball, she actually went to help Peggy up. I couldn't believe it. Now it was just me, one on one, with the Nippies' centre-forward.

Watch the player, not the ball, I thought. *Watch the player, Lily-oh. Not the ball.*

I watched her. She was a big, goofy-looking girl with curly hair and mottled pink-and-white thighs. She pulled back her leg to strike, and I heard the thunk of her boot as it struck the ball. The ball flew, high, right.

I jumped.

The ball brushed the tips of my fingers and hit the back of the net. The crowd roared. Joe Crawford smirked.

One-nil to the Nippies.

I picked the ball out of the goal and booted it back to the centre line. We played on.

*

By half-time, the score was one all. Going one down in the first minute had given us the shock we needed, and we'd actually started to play. Jess managed to find a way through the Nippies' defence and got a goal past their keeper just before the half-time whistle. We were tired, we were muddy, but we were back in the game.

'Right,' said Jess, when we were back in the changing room, massaging our calves and picking mud off our knees. 'Listen to me, girls. This is what we're going to do.'

We listened.

'The state of the pitch is awful, agreed?' she said. 'Especially around the centre spot.'

She was right. There'd been a lot of rain recently and now the sun had melted the frost, the middle of the pitch was a sea of mud. All the players were slipping and sliding about, and it was impossible to get a good kick of the ball.

'That's right. We can hardly stay on our feet.'

'If it gets much worse we'll have to dig the ball out of the mud.'

'And the wetter it gets, the heavier it gets.'

'That's the same for them though, Bella.'

'Yeah, I know, but—'

'So!' Jess interrupted, looking around at our glowing faces. 'Forwards, Polly, Else, me – we're going to play wide, right?'

'Wide? Then how—'

Jess held up a finger to stop Polly's objection. 'Wingers, drop back to give them space and help cover the defence.'

'But, Jess—'

'Trust me, Poll. It will work. Now let's go.'

I flicked a bit of mud at Peggy, who flicked it back, and then we clunked our way out of the changing room and back on to the pitch.

And, guess what? Jess's plan did work. The Nippies seemed confused by our change of tactics and kept leaving Jess and Polly unmarked, which meant they could run through the defence again and again, even though the wind was against us. It would only be a matter of time before Jess scored. Sooner or later I knew she would and I could see that Joe Crawford knew it too.

The minutes ticked by. I didn't have much to do as the play was mostly in their half. I could see Crawford getting more and more angry and impatient, and then, when there was a break in play and Jess and a few other girls went over to the touchline to get a quick drink, I saw him go up to her. I watched her standing there, her back tense and defiant, looking up at him as he spoke to her, that nasty sly grin on his face, and then, suddenly, her shoulders went limp. She turned away from him and stood looking at the ground for a moment while he walked away, hands in his pockets, a pleased swagger in his step.

The referee blew his whistle and Jess gave herself a little shake and ran back to take up her position. But there was something wrong. Her head was down and she fluffed the first two passes, letting the ball go out of play. She looked like a rag doll.

'What happened?' The Nippies were taking the throw so I had a chance to speak to Peggy. 'You were there, Peg. Did you hear what Crawford said to her?'

'Something about her brother,' said Peggy and shuddered. 'Ugh. He's a nasty piece of work, is Crawford.'

'Jess's brother?' I said. 'What about him?'

Peggy moved her eyes from the action at the

other end of the pitch and looked at me. 'You don't know?'

'What?'

'Her brother Tom, the oldest. He's in prison, for refusing to fight.'

'He's a conchie?' I couldn't believe it. I'd heard about men and boys, conscientious objectors they called them – conchies – who refused to join up and fight so got sent to prison instead, but I'd never actually known any. Men like Crawford, working in munitions, they didn't get called up. They got it easy.

'Yeah. Crawford said Jess was a loser and a coward. Just like her brother.'

A high ball came swinging towards us and Peggy moved off to boot it back up the field, leaving me standing there in the mud, rage rising in my chest, making my face burn in spite of the cold wind. Whatever reasons Jess's brother had for not wanting to fight, I was sure it wasn't because he was a coward, and it certainly wasn't Jess's fault. I looked at Crawford, standing on the touchline, hands in his pockets, laughing with another man, and I hated him like I'd never hated anyone before.

'Lil!' Peggy was screaming at me. 'Lily!'

The Nippies' centre-forward was through on goal, charging towards me, the ball at her feet, the rest of her players pushing up behind her, knowing it was their last chance to score the winning goal. I looked at the girl with the ball, and all the rage I felt at Crawford welled up inside me. As she drew back her leg to shoot I knew one thing: she would never get that ball past me. At the edge of my field of vision I saw Jess, running back to support the full-backs. I would do it for her, I thought, for my friend.

There was the hollow bang as the Nippy's boot struck the ball and sent it straight for my goal, but, just like all the times when I'd practised with Dad in the park or he'd thrown onions at me in the kitchen, or apples, to test my reflexes, I knew exactly where it was going. I launched myself into the corner of the goal and hung there in the air waiting for the ball.

I caught it. I landed. And ...

'Jess!' I yelled. 'This has got your name on it!'

I saw the flash of her grin and knew that everything was going to be all right. I threw the ball, one-handed, straight to her feet, and before anyone knew what was happening, she was off, away, galloping up the pitch with the ball at her feet. She took the shot from thirty yards away. The Nippies' keeper didn't have a chance.

The crowd roared. The whistle blew. We'd won.

As Jess hugged me and I felt her tears on my neck, and the other girls gathered round and laughed and cried and slapped each other on the back, and Billy Cracken charged on to the pitch and Dad punched the air with joy, I didn't think the day could get any better. And then, as we left the pitch, I saw the look on Joe Crawford's face and my happiness was complete.

CHAPTER ELEVEN

For a few days afterwards I woke up every morning with a feeling of happiness tucked away in a corner of my brain, like a present hidden under a bed, waiting for Christmas Day. It would take a couple of moments and then the memory would come flooding back like sunshine through the curtains: we'd won our first match, we'd beaten the Nippies, we'd shown Joe Crawford what we could do. And I'd get up and have my breakfast and then float through the day in a bubble of happiness, playing football with my friends at dinner time and pulling faces behind Joe Crawford's back from behind my machine, and I didn't think that life could get any better.

And then one day I got home from work and everything changed.

I'd been writing to Jack for a few weeks now. It wasn't easy at first, pretending to be someone else, especially when he kept asking for a photograph, but I was getting better at it. I told myself it was only what he was doing, in a way. Dad had said that soldiers weren't allowed to write about anything much to do with the war, where they were or what it was really like, so Jack was pretending too. I was sure the war wasn't all football tournaments and putting on concerts and mucking about with his friends, though I loved reading about it all. He made it almost sound like fun. Jack's best friend Harry had been a goalkeeper before the war, for Brighton, and Jack wrote funny stories about him, how he used to catch the little bombs the Germans threw over into their trenches as if they were footballs, and lob them right back to them before they exploded.

It seems like goalies are a lot more use than centre-forwards when it comes to fighting a war! Jack wrote. That made me smile, and then I thought about the bombs that Harry threw back exploding in the German trenches and I felt sick.

Jack added funny little drawings to his letters too, of himself (always with a football at his feet) his friends and the officers, and once he put a single pressed flower in the envelope, a pansy I think it was, that he'd picked from the garden of a ruined cottage somewhere and kept pressed between the pages of his notebook before sending it to me.

But today, Jack's letter was different. I snatched it up from the doormat when I got in, and then, as soon as Dad left for work, went through to the front room. I went over to the window, where I always stood to read Jack's letters, tore open the envelope and pulled out the folded sheets of notepaper. I smelt them first, like I always did, pressing them to my nose in the hope of catching a whiff of something other than paper, and then unfolded them and read quickly, my eyes gobbling up the words. It was the usual news at first, of friends and football, the marching, the cold, the dirt, the boredom, the awful food, the boredom, the boredom, the boredom. And then I got to the last page.

I'm saving the best for last, Lily Dodd. Just to see if you read my letters to the end or stop halfway through because you're so fed up with me rabbiting on about football and you've got much better things to do, like pick your teeth or have a lovely kip in front of the fire. Well. If you have read this far, I'm impressed and think you deserve to hear my news.

Are you ready? Take a deep breath and listen with both your ears . . .

Drum roll . . . da-da-da-da-da-da-da-da . . .

I'VE GOT LEAVE!

Just for a week, they're saying at the moment, but that's better than nothing. Yours truly is actually coming home. To England! To London! To YOU!!!!!!

Can we meet? Of course we can, why would you not want to see your soldier boy in the flesh? I'll tell you when, you tell me where, and we will have the best day ever!

From your friend

Jack

I folded up the sheets and put them back in the envelope, then rested my forehead against the cool glass of the window and stared at my not-pretty face, floating in the blackness outside.

Now what?

I don't know how long I stood like that, wondering what to do, before I heard it. Someone was hammering at the door. They sounded impatient, as if they'd been knocking for a long time, so I shoved Jack's letter in my pocket and went through to the hall, trying to ignore the worried voice in my head. Who could it be? People banging on the door at night was never good news. There were often accidents at the Arsenal, it was a dangerous place to work. What if something had happened to Dad?

It was Billy Cracken.

'Bill?' His face looked blue in the dim light of the street lamp, and I was afraid.

'You've got to come, Lil,' he said. His voice was shaking. My stomach clenched.

'Why? What's happened?'

'They've hit a Zep, out over the estuary!'

I realized it was excitement that was making his voice shake. The Zeppelins didn't come that often, and for a while they'd stopped coming altogether. They mostly sent planes now, big ones loaded up with bombs – Giants, they were called – but somehow they didn't seem as bad as the huge bloated Zeppelins. I could never quite believe they were built and operated by people, they seemed like monsters from a dream. One dropped a bomb on a school across the river from us in Poplar, in broad daylight, when the children were there, and some of them were killed. It was terrible. But the bombers mostly came at night, and they liked it best when the moon was full so they could see just what they were aiming for. I hated them for that.

'They say it's on fire, Lil!' said Billy. 'Come on!'

It wasn't too cold, so I went straight out without stopping to put on a coat. Doors were opening all down the street as the news spread and people came hurrying out of their houses – women in their slippers, boys chasing each other, big girls holding the hands of little ones, old men with sticks, complaining at the fuss, but still wanting to see what was happening. More and more people joined the crowd as we all made our way across

Beresford Square and down to the river.

And there it was. Hanging in the air over the marshes where the river widened out, the great airship, blazing orange and red like a huge glowing flower against the navy blue of the night sky. Billy and I stood there along with hundreds of others, our faces turned up to the sky, glowing pink and orange with the light from the blazing airship. I saw boys I knew from school in the crowd, and girls from work. Even Miss Barker was there, with a friend, looking quite small and ordinary without her uniform. The whole of Woolwich – the whole of London, it seemed – had come out to watch the German airship burn. And then:

WHOOSH!

Another part of the airship caught and blazed up and a huge cheer went up that seemed to come from all over London. I reached for Billy's hand, I don't know why, and then I felt embarrassed and wished I hadn't but didn't know how to let go.

There were little bits of flame falling down from the airship towards the river, like petals falling from a flower or leaves from a tree at the end of summer. 'What are they?' I said to nobody in particular. 'Bits of the airship?'

Billy said nothing, but an old man standing next to us took his cigarette out of his mouth and spat thoughtfully on the ground.

'No, love,' he said and pushed back his cap to scratch his head, his eyes still on the sky. 'Those are never bits of airship. Those are men. German airmen. On fire.'

As he spoke another fluttered down and I saw that he was right. I could just make out the arms and legs of a man, black in the middle of the fire. I suddenly felt cold and was glad of Billy's hand, warm and a bit sticky, in mine. I squeezed it and he squeezed back. Everyone else in the crowd seemed to realize at the same time that those burning fragments were not bits of airship but actual human beings, with mums and dads and friends and children who loved them, because the cheers became half-hearted and then stopped completely. There was no sound but the ever-present throb of the Arsenal behind us and the roar of the burning Zeppelin and we all just stood there, faces turned up to the sky, watching those little burning fragments flutter silently down like dying butterflies.

Next to me the old man was shaking his head, and a woman who had been holding her baby up to watch rubbed her face on the baby's back to wipe away a tear. Perhaps she had a husband in France, fighting men like the ones who were falling in flames from our London sky. And even though those men were trying to kill him, to leave her a widow, her baby without a father, still she couldn't feel glad to see those Germen airmen die.

'Let's go,' I said. Billy nodded and we joined the others who were beginning to drift away, back to their homes, their kitchens, their beds. Nobody said a word. Nobody even looked at each other. It was as if we'd all been part of something which had made us feel ashamed.

That night I dreamt of Jack. I dreamt we were out on the marshes together, near the place where the Zeppelin had burnt. It was a soft summer night full of stars. We'd been walking, and we stopped and looked out over the river where the mist and the moonlight were all tangled up together, and Jack turned to me and touched my face, and we looked at each other. That was all.

When the alarm clock shattered my dream, I

woke up feeling perfectly happy, as if the night before had never happened. Then I remembered, and remembered I had to go to work, packing ammunition that would kill boys like Jack and men like my dad. And I remembered that Jack was coming home on leave, and that he wanted to meet me, and I didn't know what to do.

CHAPTER TWELVE

It was the following night, and I was walking home from the factory, more tired than I'd ever been before. It was getting dark and the whole of Woolwich was shrouded in a gritty yellow fog that stuck in your throat and wrapped itself around the buildings like a grimy scarf. I'd been moved into the packing room, putting bullets into cases, which was even more boring than the work I'd been doing on the grinding machine, and although it was miles and miles away from the friends I'd made in the machine room, Crawford still went out of his way to find me and make my life miserable.

The lamps were already gleaming through the fog that swirled around the dark shapes of the stalls and barrows in Beresford Square, and the men's voices, calling to each other through the murk, sounded like voices in a dream. How was I going to tell Jack that I couldn't meet him when he came home on leave? I'd been pretending to be someone I wasn't, someone little and pretty with soft fair curls. The type of girl who laughed at his jokes rather than wanting him to laugh at mine. The type of girl who didn't play football. I didn't think any amount of lovely hair would make up for the fact that I'd lied to him about who I really was.

'Hey, Lily! Lily of Laguna!'

A smiling face loomed out of the fog.

'Mr Singh! Hello. Are you well?'

Mr Singh's market stall had been there as long as I could remember. It was between the pet stall, with its lovebirds and squawking parrots, and the flower stall, where old Mrs Pinker sold lilac and violets, carnations smelling of cloves, roses and lilies from green metal buckets. Mr Singh sold ribbons and embroidered shawls and beautiful bright silks, all the way from India, he used to tell us. When Amy May and I were little we used to sigh over them, feeling the ribbons between our fingers, stroking the silks and dreaming of the day when we'd be grown-up ladies who could afford to have dresses made in green and gold and scarlet. We'd stay there until Mr Singh told us off for getting greasy finger marks on his wares and shooed us away.

But now he was smiling at me. 'Not too bad, not too bad,' he replied. 'All the better for seeing you, my dear.' He bent down and picked up a rose that was lying in the gutter, next to some rotten potatoes and a cabbage stalk. It was yellow and quite perfect. Mrs Pinker must've dropped it when she was packing up her stall. An out-of-season rose, grown in some hothouse somewhere. Mr Singh presented it to me with a little bow. 'A rose for a Lily,' he said and bowed again, his hand on his heart, before disappearing into the fog.

'Thank you,' I called after him. 'It's lovely.' But he was gone.

I smelt the rose, sticking my nose right into its petals and breathing in its appley scent. Then I tucked it in the front of my coat where I could smell it all the way home.

*

'Hello-o-o!'

Dad was in the kitchen, rinsing out his teacup before leaving for his night shift.

'Letter from France, Lily-oh,' he said. 'Not the usual writing. I'm thinking perhaps ...'

I looked at him. He looked back.

'Amy,' I said.

He nodded. 'That's what I thought. Hoped.'

The letter was lying on the table, next to the breadboard with the remains of the loaf.

Dad was watching me. 'Is it her writing?'

I nodded and looked at the mad, oversized loopy writing that covered the back of the envelope. *To:* it said, with a little line drawn underneath. Then my name in huge great capitals: *MISS LILY DODD.* Next came the address, the writing so big that the space ran out and *ANGLETERRE* had to be squeezed in at the end in tiny little letters.

Dad looked at the clock. 'Oops, I best get off,' he said, grabbing his jacket from the back of the door. 'There's cheese in the cupboard, and Stan-next-door gave me some eggs, so you can make yourself an omelette. Don't stay up too late.'

'I won't,' I said and looked back at the envelope. Then, suddenly—

FWOOOOOOSH!

Something flew past my shoulder. Dad had grabbed an apple on his way out and sent it spinning straight for me. I caught it (of course I did) just by sticking out one hand, and turned to see Dad laughing at me from the doorway. I lobbed it back to him and he caught it easily like a cricket ball.

'Good work, Lily-oh,' he said. 'We'll be top of the league before you know it, you'll see.' Then he took a bite out of the apple, tipped his cap to me and was gone.

The front door slammed as I tore open the envelope. There was the address first, somewhere in France I'd never heard of, and then:

Sorry sorry sorry sorry sorry sorry!!!!!!!!
Sorry I haven't written before! Were you worried? Did you think I was killed or injured or fallen in love with a French boy? (ha!) Or, worst of all, that I wasn't your Best Friend any more (oh ha, ha and ha!)?????
Well, hard cheese, Lily Dodd, because I am here, I

am in one piece, I am still your best friend and I am a NURSE!!!! In FRANCE!!!!!!

Well, almost a nurse. I'm actually an ORDERLY which means a sort of helper for the proper nurses. They don't let me do any of the good stuff like bandaging wounds or helping with the operations (There's a LADY SURGEON here who looks just like Miss Hogweed! You know, with that long thin nose that runs down her face like a drip of water?) You have to do lots more training to be a proper nurse and I was in such a hurry to get out here and HELP that I didn't want to wait.

That made me smile. Amy was always in a hurry.

So what does Amy May do then, I hear you ask, if she's not a proper nurse? Well! What I mostly do is make tea, make beds, mop floors, strip beds, wash bandages, serve tea, empty bedpans, wash bedpans, make more tea, make more beds, get ordered about and talk to the soldiers (the ones that CAN talk of course). That's the best bit, talking to the boys, and oh Lily, there's so so so so many. And they're from all over the place, Scotland, India. Australia! (hardly seems worth it to come all that way just to get shot at by Germans and then get looked after by ME, does it?) I met one from Yorkshire the other day!

Yorkshire? Jess had told me there were some really good ladies' teams up there.

We even have a few German soldiers, which I think is v nice of us, seeing as they started the whole thing, ha de ha. Though I expect they think WE started it and anyway we could hardly refuse to bandage them up when they arrive here all hurt and bleeding, could we? And they seem nice, but it's quite hard to say because they can't speak English and I can't speak German, except for one word they taught me to say which I think must be rude because they keep asking me to repeat it and then when I do they laugh and laugh until they start coughing and one of the sisters (they're the nurses in charge and they're ALL like Miss Hogweed – looking at you like you've just made a bad smell and BOSSY-BOOTS BOSSY-BOOTS BOSSY-BOSSY-BOSSY-BOOTS) comes in and tells them off.

One of the VADs (they're the volunteer nurses, don't know why they're called that. The men say it stands for Very Adorable Darlings, but that can't be right, can it?), she used to go on holidays to Germany (WHY OH WHY?) when she was a little girl (her family must be RICH), so she can speak German and she talks to the German soldiers. There's one of them who looks at me with big sad brown eyes like a puppy dog and the VAD told me he asked her what my name was!

HA, HA AND HA!

But, Lily Dodd, I haven't said what my big news is, which is that I am COMING HOME! I've got leave in a couple of weeks, not quite sure exactly, but will let you know. Will you come to meet me at Waterloo station? Please, please, please, oh PLEASE! Because I have another BIG SURPRISE and I want you to be the first to know, partly because I can't tell Mum and Dad because they'd go stark raving bonkers if I did!!!!!!

What on earth? I thought. What has she gone and done now? I read on to the end of the letter.

Will send telegram when I know when I'm coming all right?

Love to my BEST BEST FRIEND from her BEST BEST FRIEND

AMY MAY PLINK PLONK xxxxxxxxxxx

I put the letter back in its envelope and stood there for a minute, listening to the tick of the kitchen clock. Outside the hooter from the Arsenal boomed through the fog, calling the people into work for the night shift. I thought of Dad and the others trudging in through Number Four Gate as the last few stragglers left to go home after the day shift, home to food and family and sleep. All over Woolwich, front doors were slamming and people were looking up from their work and listening to voices in hallways:

'I'm ho-o-ome!'

Home, I thought, looking round the little kitchen. The stained sink and the dripping tap and Dad's teacup upside down on the wooden draining board. I put the envelope down on the table and thought of the other letter I'd got that week, the one hidden away in the biscuit tin under my bed upstairs.

Amy's coming home, said the voice in my head, *after all this time my best friend's coming home.*

And she wasn't the only one.

CHAPTER THIRTEEN

I hadn't expected the streets to be so busy at that time of night. All along Waterloo Road there were ambulances, lined up two deep in some places, and crowds of people – women and girls mostly – huddled in anxious little groups, or walking stiff-backed and alone towards the station.

I got off the tram and let myself be swept along by the crowd. Closer to the station there were more and more soldiers, standing around, sitting on the steps, men in khaki with packs on their backs and rifles, some with women leaning on their arms. One had a little girl on his shoulders, looking around wide-eyed at all the people and playing with his hair, just as if they were off for a day trip to the seaside. The men were mostly silent and stony-faced, the women smiling smiles that looked like they could turn to tears at any moment. Some men had flowers in their button-holes, pink roses against khaki tunics, grabbed at the last minute from suburban gardens. One even had a whole bunch of flowers tied to his rifle with a piece of string. There were young girls in their best clothes and women carrying babies, tense with excitement and fear, their faces gleaming white in the dusk. They were like me, I guessed, going to meet someone they loved who was coming home.

Inside the station it was even more crowded. Groups of soldiers were sitting and lying on the ground, leaning on their packs, their rifles piled up in the middle like a campfire waiting to be lit. Some seemed to be asleep and some just lay there, staring up at the pigeons that were making slow circles in the smoke that hung under the station's high glass roof. Somewhere a woman's laugh, high and false-sounding, cut through the gloom, and an engine released a great sigh of steam.

I looked up at the clock that hung over us, ticking away the time. Nearly eight o'clock; Amy's train was due. I went over to the platform but there was no sign of any train, just a few people like me hanging around, not knowing what to do, so I wandered off again. Lamps had been lit around the station now, casting a blue light through the gloom and making the silent huddles of people look like grey ghosts waiting at the edge of time. Every now and again there'd be a hoot as a train crawled in and people would surge forward, hoping, hoping, hoping and then retreat, disappointed when it turned out to be a false alarm. The hospital trains all came in at the same platform, where the ambulances were able to drive right into the station and collect their loads of limping, bandaged men and humped bodies on stretchers and drive them away to get better or to die. I'd never felt so close to the war before. The guns, the bullets, the shells we made at the Arsenal were just things. They didn't seem real, not like this. This was people.

The goodbyes were mostly silent. Couples clung to each other and then pulled apart and walked off in different directions as if they were in a hurry. Nobody ever looked back. Sometimes they whispered to each other, and once, as I stopped at a stall to buy a cup of tea and a bun, a woman's scream cut though the air before dying away into silence like a spent firework. The sound seemed to go straight through me, but most people didn't react. Some shrugged and shook their heads with something like disapproval as if they felt the poor woman had somehow let us all down by allowing her agony to escape in that ghastly howl.

I leant against a pillar. I drank my tea. I ate my bun. It was half past eight. Then nine. At half past nine I went to check. Still no train at platform four. I found a porter who was staring up at the departures board and scratching his head.

'I'm meeting a friend,' I said, then stopped, feeling stupid.

The porter gave a tired smile and pushed his cap back on his head, his eyes resting on a family standing nearby in a worried little huddle. He must have heard the same thing a hundred times that day, but his look was kind.

'Do you know what train he's on, love? Where's he coming from?'

'She,' I said. I don't know why it felt important to tell him that, but it did. 'It's my best friend. She's a nurse, should be on the train from Southampton.'

He nodded again and looked up at the clock. 'There's a few due in tonight,' he said. 'Mostly running late as usual. You'll have to wait and see.'

'Thanks,' I said and went back to my pillar. Ten o'clock came and went and I started to worry about getting home. The trams and the Tube would stop running at midnight. I wandered off and found a stall selling a few sad-looking flowers, where I bought a bunch of carnations. I was paying the woman when I heard a voice behind me.

'They wouldn't be for me, would they, Lily Dodd?'

I turned. I dropped my purse and my money went spinning across the ground. She was there. My Amy May was there. She was alive, she was in one piece and she was there.

And she had something buttoned into the front of her coat. Something that moved.

It was a dog. Amy May had come all the way back from France with a dog stuffed down the front of her coat. It was a very small dog, about the size of a football boot, but even so. It was still a dog and it was still down the front of her coat. She really was unbelievable.

'It's a present,' she said when she saw what I was staring at. 'All the way from France.' She did one of her smiles. 'For you.'

And then she pulled the dog out of her jacket and held him out to me with both hands as if he was a bunch of flowers. He wasn't much more than a puppy, with wiry white fur, a shiny black nose and one black ear. He looked at me, his back legs hanging down, and wagged a stumpy tail.

'I can't have a dog, Amy.'

'Well, I can't take him back to France, and Mum won't have him. And, Lil! Look how sweet he is!'

'Where did you get him?' I said, trying to pretend I wasn't really interested.

'Some soldiers passing through on their way home. They'd found him in the ruins of a village on their way back from the front and left him with us, poor little scrap. Look, Lil!' She held the dog up and made him wave his paw like a puppet. 'Hello, Lily Dodd!' she said, doing his voice. 'My name's Wilfred and I lo-o-ove you!'

I laughed. I couldn't help it. 'Is that really what he's called?' I said. 'Wilfred?'

'It's what the men called him. Suits him, doesn't it?' It did. Amy saw I was softening. 'Go on,' she said. 'Give him a scratch. You know you want to.'

She was right, I did want to, so I reached out a hand and touched the puppy's head. I could feel the hardness of his skull under the velvety softness of his fur. He wagged his tail again.

'He likes you,' said Amy. 'I knew he would. And I knew you'd agree to have him in the end.'

And so Amy May got her way as usual, and I became a dog owner. We went back to Woolwich together watching the darkness rattle past the windows of the tram as it lurched around the rain-streaked streets. Amy did most of the talking and Wilfred sat on my lap, his small body feeling warm and heavy against my legs. She talked so much that I nearly forgot to tell her about Jack, how he was coming home on leave and wanted to meet me and how I was scared that if he did he wouldn't want to write to me any more. And when I told her, my friend stopped talking and turned in her seat to look at me. The blue light from the dim street lamps was passing over her little face and I suddenly felt so glad to see her that I wanted to cry.

'Lily Dodd,' she said after a pause, 'that is the daftest thing I've ever heard in my life. Why would this boy not want to write to you any more after you'd met?'

'Because,' I said and shrugged.

'Because what? Because he's an *idiot*?'

'No! He's nice! And funny and brave. But—'

'But?'

'He's handsome! All right? He's very, very handsome.' The words tumbled out before I could stop them. 'He's really really nice-looking, Amy, and I'm . . .'

'What? You're what, Lil?'

'Not,' I said quietly. 'I'm not.' I glared at her, daring her to deny it, to tell me I was nice-looking even though we both knew I was a not-pretty girl with feet so big they could fit into her dad's football boots. But she didn't, so I said, 'He doesn't know I play football either.'

'You said he was in the Footballers' Battalion!'

'Yes, but boys don't like it, though, do they? Girls playing football.' I knew I was just repeating what Dora Crawford had said, but I said it anyway.

'Getting all hot and dirty. Showing their knees. It's hardly ladylike, is it?'

Amy stared. 'Who told you that?' she said. 'And don't say nobody, because someone did. That's not you talking, Lil. Since when have you cared about being ladylike?'

'Since I've been writing to Jack. I like him, Amy, I really, really like him. And . . . I couldn't bear it if he didn't want to write to me any more.'

A fat tear dropped on to Wilfred's head. Amy put a hand on my arm. Her eyes had their old excited glitter.

'Write to him,' she said. 'Tell him you'll meet him.'

I opened my mouth to speak but she held up her hand to stop me.

'I,' she said, 'have got a very good idea.'

'Right,' said Amy. 'This is what we're going to do.'

It was the next day and we were in our favourite spot on Plumstead Marshes, lying on an old rug I'd brought from home and staring up at a white wintry sky. I propped myself on one elbow and looked at her.

'What do you mean, we?' I said and flicked her nose.

'Ow! I mean you, Lil. Us. But mostly you.' She rolled over so we were lying face to face. 'You write a letter to your Jack Darling. Tell him you'll meet him when he's home on leave.' I opened my mouth to object, but she carried on. 'Where would be a good place for a nice day out with your best boy?'

'Amy—'

'The zoo!' she shouted suddenly. 'You could meet him at the zoo!'

Neither of us had ever been to the zoo in Regent's Park, but we'd longed to ever since we were little. Dad and Mum had been once when they were courting. He'd told me that she'd pretended to be scared of the tigers, but he knew it was just to give him an excuse to put his arm round her.

'Lily!' Amy's voice interrupted my thoughts. 'Are you listening to me?'

She was sitting up on the rug, looking down at me, and I suddenly knew. Amy's Big Idea. It was so obvious that I couldn't believe it had taken me so long to work out.

'No,' I said. 'Amy, no. You're not saying...'

'Yup,' she said. 'You write to your Jack Darling.

You tell him you'll meet him at the zoo. Well, outside the zoo, at the main gate. I think it's right that he pays, don't you?'

'Amy—'

'You give him a day. A time. Ten o'clock? Yes, that sounds good, then you can have a lovely long day together, looking at the animals, pretending to be frightened of the tigers,' (how did she know about that? I supposed I must have told her the story about my mum and dad) 'having a nice cup of tea, ice cream, getting to know each other a little bit, but not too much, if you know what I mean.' She turned to me, her funny eyes sparkling. 'Doesn't that sound lovely, Lil? Doesn't it sound like a perfectly lovely day?'

'It does,' I said. 'It sounds really lovely. But the only thing is that it won't be me, will it? It'll be you.'

After we left the marshes, Amy and I walked back to Spray Street so she could help me write the letter. This is what I wrote:

Dear Jack,
Well! Your leave is coming up in no time! I would

*like to meet you and hope you would still like to meet
me. If so, it will have to be on the Sunday of your
leave, the day before you go back. Is that all right? It
is my only day off, see. Well, I have Saturday afternoon* (which was for football training with Dad
and the girls from their Rockets, but I wasn't going
to tell him that) *but it would be nice to have a whole
day together so we can really get to know each other.*
(That bit was Amy's idea. I wouldn't have been so
forward.) *If this is all right with you I will be at the
main entrance of the zoo at ten o'clock. You will
know it is me because I will be wearing a bunch of
violets in my coat and looking very excited because I
have never been to the zoo before!* (That last bit was
Amy's idea too. It didn't really sound like me, but it
was going to be her Jack met, so it didn't seem to
matter.)

*Will you let me know if this is all right? And if
your leave is going ahead as planned of course.*

Hoping this finds you in the pink

From

Your friend

Lily Dodd

Jack's reply came a few days later. He'd be there, he said. He couldn't wait to meet me, he said. I didn't need to wear violets for him to know me, he said. He'd know me the moment he set eyes on me, he said. He'd just be looking out for the prettiest girl in the world.

Oh. Oh. Oh.

CHAPTER FOURTEEN

'What's wrong, love?'

I'd woken up with the dirty London light seeping though my bedroom curtains and a sick feeling in my stomach. I splashed my face with cold water and went downstairs to find Dad in the kitchen feeding Wilfred. They'd taken to each other straight away. Dad had always loved dogs – he used to keep terriers as a boy – and I'd never seen a look on his face like the one when I got home that night from Waterloo station with a new puppy under my arm.

Dad put Wilfred's dish down on the floor and turned to me with a grin that quickly faded. 'Lil?' he said. 'Is something the matter?'

'No,' I said and sat down at the table. How could

I have agreed to this? How could I have thought it was a good idea to let Amy pretend to be me? I thought of her getting up in the tiny bedroom she had to herself at the back of her house and getting ready for her day out with my boy. I pictured her washing her face and brushing her hair, putting on her stockings and her Sunday suit and then taking the bunch of violets that we'd bought at the market the night before and pinning them to the front of her coat.

I couldn't bear it.

Dad rubbed his hands together. 'Well,' he said. 'As it's Sunday I thought I'd take our Wilf for a good long tramp on the marshes. D'you want to come?'

'No, thanks, Dad,' I said. 'I'm a bit tired. Think I'll just, you know, rest a bit before work tomorrow.'

Dad knew by my face that something was wrong, but he also knew better than to ask me what it was. He reached for his old coat and muffler, wrapping the scarf around his face. He'd been complaining of a twinge in one of his teeth recently. I told him he'd have to go and see the old man at the market who pulled teeth for sixpence, but Dad had made a face and said he'd rather do it himself the old-fashioned way, with a bit of string and a door knob. I watched him as he arranged the scarf carefully around his face to keep the cold away from his poorly tooth, and I had an idea.

'Sure you don't want to come?' he said, his voice a bit muffled by the scarf. 'You look like you could do with a breath of fresh air.'

'No, Dad, it's fine. You go.'

'Please yourself,' he said, taking his cap from the hook on the back of the door and pulling it well down over his ears. You couldn't see much of his face at all now, just his nose and his eyes looking out from under his cap. 'We'll see you later.'

He took Wilfred's new lead from the same hook and clipped it on to his collar. Then, as he straightened up, he added, 'I said I'd go over to Silvertown to see your Aunty Nora later on, so we'll be out all day.'

'All right, Dad.'

He hesitated for a moment, looking at me, while the little dog strained at the lead, desperate to get out on the marshes and pretend to chase rabbits. 'Come on, Wilf,' he said. The door slammed and they were gone.

I looked at the clock. It was still early, a quarter past eight. If I moved fast I could do it.

I went to Dad's room first, the one he'd shared with Mum, at the front of the house. I never usually liked going in there. The bed had space for two people, but there was only one pillow, on the side nearest the door. The other side was empty. The room smelt of Dad now, of tobacco and engine oil and the stuff he put on his hair. I wondered what it would have smelt like if Mum was still there.

I hurried over to the chest opposite the bed and pulled open the top drawer. Empty. Nothing but a faint smell of lavender and a yellowed slip of paper at the back that had some numbers written on it. It must've been Mum's. The next drawer just had some underwear of Dad's, socks, nothing I could use. The wardrobe. This was better, I rummaged, looking for old things, things that wouldn't be missed.

Trousers. An old pair, frayed at the edges, holes in both front pockets. A shirt. No collar. That didn't matter, it was Sunday but nobody went to

Waltham Forest Libraries and Information

Customer name: Nazir, Adil
Customer ID: *****163617

Items that you have borrowed

Title: The death of all things seen
ID: 90400000475842
Due: 09 November 2019

Total items: 1
Account balance: £0.00
19/10/2019 14:14
Borrowed 4
Overdue: 0
Hold requests: 0
Ready for collection: 0

Thank you for using Self-Service
Need to renew your books?
www.londonlibraries.gov.uk/walthamforest or
dial 020 8496 3000 - available 24/7.
You will need your library card and PIN, please
speak to a member of staff.

church these days, the war had put them off it. An ancient jacket that Dad hadn't worn for years. I went through to my room with my finds and put them on. The trousers were much too big round the waist, but I used one of my belts to hold them up. Then I looked in the mirror. And stared.

I looked taller, if that was possible. Slimmer, straighter, stronger. Prettier, somehow. But most of all, more like . . . me.

What about my hair? I'd never had it cut in my life and the heavy plait hung down below my waist. There was far too much to hide beneath a cap, so I tucked it down the back of the shirt, where it tickled. Then I pulled one of Dad's old caps down over my head and wound a scarf around my neck and face, like he did to protect his tooth from the cold, and looked at my reflection again.

I would do.

Amy had never liked the Tube, said it made her feel funny being underground, so I reckoned she'd take the tram. I didn't want to risk bumping into her so I set off for the train station as fast as I could, striding along with no skirts flapping round my legs to slow me up. I bought my ticket, got on the first train to London Bridge and sat down, amongst the crowds of people going home after their night shifts, the men in uniform and the families going out for the day, feeling like everybody must know I was a girl dressed up in my dad's old clothes. But nobody looked at me, nobody stared, nobody seemed to notice anything strange about me at all, except for one little girl who fixed me with a suspicious glare, but then held up her dolly to wave to me behind her mother's back when we all got off the train at London Bridge.

Now what? I didn't know how to get to the zoo, so I found a friendly-looking guard.

'Excuse me—' I said, then stopped. The guard looked startled, and I remembered I was meant to be a boy. 'I want to get to the zoo,' I said in a voice so deep that it sounded silly, and I nearly laughed thinking about what Amy would say if she could hear me.

It can't have sounded silly to the guard though, because he just said, 'Great Portland Street, son.' (*Son!*) 'Change at Moorgate for the Metropolitan Line. Cross the road and walk up through the park, you can't miss it.'

'Thanks,' I said, so relieved to get away with it that I forgot to do the deep voice.

I felt his eyes on my back as I hurried away, as pleased with myself as the day we'd beaten the Nippies at the old Manor Ground. There was a train waiting when I got to the platform, so I got on and sat down opposite a girl of about my age who actually blushed and looked away when I caught her eye. I wasn't just a boy, I thought. I was a boy that girls fancied! As the train moved off, I kept thinking how impressed Amy would be when I told her what I'd done – she was usually the one who did things like this. Then I remembered that I was doing it so I could spy on her, and that was something we'd never be able to share.

By the time I'd got off at the right station and hurried across the park, past the boys playing football and the rich people pointing at rose bushes, and arrived at the zoo's main entrance, it was nearly ten o'clock and I'd half forgotten why I'd come. And then I saw her. Little Amy May, so sweet and so pretty, standing by the gate in her best Sunday clothes with the violets tucked in the front of her coat. She wasn't looking in my direction, but I stepped behind a tree to keep out of sight just in case. *Is he late?* I thought. *He can't be late! Surely a gentleman should make sure he arrives first.*

And then: 'Lily?'

The voice came from behind me. I turned, forgetting for a moment that I wasn't Lily. And there he was. The boy in my photograph. He looked a bit older and a lot more tired, but he was still tall and curly-haired and handsome, so handsome, in his uniform.

'Lily Dodd!'

Amy must've forgotten who she was supposed to be too, because she looked startled. Then, as he strode towards her, passing so close to me that I could have reached out and touched him, I saw her remember and she straightened her face into a smile. I hid my face as he went past, looking at the pavement and watching his boots. They were old and worn but newly polished, shining conker-brown like my dad's football boots, the ones that were now mine. *He's polished them this morning*, I thought. *He's polished them for me.* But it wasn't for me, was it? It was for her.

I peered around my tree and saw him reach her. I couldn't hear what they said, I was too far away, but I saw him hesitate for a second, looking at her in a slightly puzzled way. Then she smiled and said something, and they shook hands and went off together towards the ticket office.

He paid for both of them, just like Amy said he would, and they went in. I waited until they were out of sight and then I went up and bought my ticket.

CHAPTER FIFTEEN

I went through the turnstile and looked around for Amy and Jack, making sure I stayed out of sight. The zoo was quite empty – it was probably too early in the day for most people. There were no families with children running around begging for sweets and elephant rides, no nursemaids pushing prams or couples snatching a precious few moments together away from the war. Apart from a sad-looking keeper sweeping up dead leaves, it seemed like I had the whole place to myself.

Then I spotted them, walking along one of the paths that led away from the entrance. They looked awkward and a bit embarrassed, him so tall and her so little, walking side by side but a bit apart so they wouldn't brush against each other by accident. I could see Amy's bright little face, turned up to his, asking him questions, laughing at his replies. She'd always been good at talking to boys. Jack wasn't saying much, just nodding and smiling, his cap under his arm. I could tell he was a footballer. His back was broad and flat in his uniform and he moved easily, with long strides that he had to shorten so Amy could keep up with him. *He wouldn't have to do that with me*, I thought. *My legs are as long as his, longer perhaps.* But he wasn't with me, was he? He was with Amy.

After a minute, I set off after them, making my way along the path past cages of strange-looking birds that screamed and squawked and a small, scruffy-looking monkey whose eyes followed me as I went past. I wasn't very interested in the birds, but I'd never seen a monkey, not a real one, so I stopped for a second to say hello. His eyes were an orangey-brown colour, the same as mine, and they looked kind and sad, but I couldn't wait. Jack and Amy had kept going and I wasn't going to let them out of my sight.

And then I did.

They'd disappeared around a bend in the path up ahead, but when I turned the corner they were nowhere to be seen. I'd come to a sort of cross-roads, with three paths leading off in different directions and a little signpost pointing to various places: the entrance, the tearoom, the reptile house. I didn't know which way to go, so decided to take the one to the reptile house as that sounded most interesting. I hurried along past flowerbeds that contained nothing but mud and snails until I spotted them, outside a big brick building at the end of the path. Jack was holding open a door for Amy to go inside, and then he followed her, so both of them were swallowed up by the darkness beyond the door.

I ran up, my boots sounding loud on the path. The words REPTILE HOUSE were picked out above the doorway in big stone letters. I pushed open the door and went in, standing out of sight behind an iron pillar by the entrance. It was dark inside, so dark that it took some time for my eyes to get used to the gloom, and there was a strange musty smell like nothing I'd ever smelt before. I looked around. Reptiles. That meant snakes, didn't it? Snakes and lizards, things like that. I shuddered and looked around for Jack and Amy.

It was their footsteps I heard first, echoing in the gloom, then Amy's giggle. She and Jack were at the far end of the long room (it reminded me of the workshops at the Arsenal) looking at something in one of the cages. I stayed behind my pillar to keep out of sight, but there was no need. They weren't looking in my direction. They were looking at each other. Amy was talking a lot now, waving her hands about, touching her hair and looking up at Jack, laughing into his eyes. And he was laughing back. He didn't look awkward any more. He looked like he was having fun.

I couldn't bear it, so I turned away and found myself looking into a murky yellow eye with a vertical pupil like a cat's. But it didn't gleam like a cat's eye. It was milky-looking, opaque and dull, like the eye of a dead fish on a stall in the market. A crocodile. I didn't think it was real at first, it was so huge and so still, lying there on the floor of its cage, like a great tree trunk washed up on some faraway beach. I'd always thought crocodiles were green but this one was a dull greyish-brown, the exact colour of the Arsenal mud and its skin looked dry and scratchy. Only its teeth were white, poking out at random from the long grinning mouth. The grin seemed to widen as I stared at it, as if the crocodile knew exactly why I was there and what I was thinking. I told myself that was silly. How could a crocodile know what I was thinking? It probably didn't even know I was there.

And then it winked. It did. The crocodile winked at me.

Amy's giggle echoed in the gloom. I peered around the pillar. She was brushing something off the front of Jack's tunic, and then she took his cap from him and put it on her own head, striking a little pose. I felt sick. And when I looked back at the crocodile its grin seemed to have got even wider. *She likes him*, the grin seemed to be saying. Then I heard Jack's laugh, a warm, low chuckle. *And it sounds as if he likes her too.*

I felt a deep twang inside my chest and my stomach seemed to clench itself into a tight little knot. Amy laughed again. I heard her say something. Her light voice twinkled through the darkness, but I couldn't catch the words. I screwed up my eyes. I didn't want to see this, I didn't.

Have a look, the crocodile said. Its ancient voice creaked in my head like an old iron door. *Go on, take another peek. See what they're up to. The pair of them. The naughties!*

I shook my head, feeling the heavy plait of my hair moving against the skin of my back under Dad's shirt. *No*, I thought. *I don't want to. I just want to be back at home in Spray Street or walking on the marshes with Dad and Wilfred with the cold wind on my face. I should never have come. This is awful.*

Go on, said the crocodile. *You don't want to miss anything. Not after you've come all this way. Go on, look.*

And so, as if a string was pulling my head in their direction, I turned and looked. Amy and Jack had sat down together on a bench. They had their backs to me, and his dark head and her fair one were close together, side by side. Their shoulders were touching. I rested my face against the iron pillar. It felt cold against my hot cheek. The air in the room seethed and hummed and snakes slithered silently in the dark. I heard the faint screech of a bird or a monkey outside. I watched and I waited. Something was going to happen.

Amy was laughing and talking, her little face glittering in the gloom, while Jack replied slowly and carefully, his voice a deep rumble that I felt in the pit of my stomach. I couldn't see his face. But as I watched, Amy reached up and touched his cheek, turning his face to hers. And then she kissed him. She did. She kissed him on the mouth.

The room swayed. I held on to the pillar. For a moment I thought I was actually going to be sick. I turned away, staggering, not knowing what to do. *What now?* my brain screamed at me. *What do I do now?*

Go, said the voice in my head.

I looked at the crocodile.

Just leave, walk away, it said in its creaky voice. *Leave them, they're happy together. They don't want you.*

I heard Amy's giggle again, and then her voice, and the low rumble of Jack's replies.

Listen to that, said the crocodile. *They're talking about you now, I expect. She's telling him the truth. How she's not really you. How you're not little or pretty or sweet like her. You're a not-pretty girl of five foot ten with feet big enough to fit into her dad's football boots.*

Amy's laugh tinkled in the darkness.

Hear that? said the crocodile. *They're laughing about it. Laughing at you.*

What shall I do? I thought. *What can I do?*

Go, said the crocodile again. *Leave them to it! Hold your hatred and your anger close to your heart, roll it up into a tight little knot in your stomach and carry it home with you. Carry it with you always,* said the voice. *That'll show them. Show them you don't need them. You don't care.*

So I did.

I turned and left the Reptile House, stumbling out into the gritty London daylight, and marched blindly back the way I'd come to the main entrance of the zoo. The birds screamed harsh, mocking laughs as I passed their cages, but I didn't look at them. I didn't stop to see the monkey, and when I got to the turnstile I went straight out. The man in the ticket booth called something after me, but I didn't stop. I walked across the park, then got back on the Tube and sat there, feeling hot and ashamed and stupid in my dad's old clothes.

By the time I got back to Woolwich I'd convinced myself the crocodile was right. Amy would have told him everything. I pictured them together at the zoo, her and Jack, looking at the tigers – Amy pretending to be scared so he'd put his arm round her – laughing at the monkeys, riding on the elephant. She would tell him how she and I were friends and how I'd been too scared to meet him because of being so tall and so not-pretty, so she'd gone in my place. And he'd look serious at first and then he'd put one finger under her chin to tilt her head up to his and he'd look straight into her odd-coloured eyes and he'd say, 'I'm glad you did it. Because it meant that we met, you and me.'

Then she'd tell him her real name, and how she was a nurse in France, not a boring old factory worker like me, and he'd say that perhaps they might manage to meet up over there, go to a café or something and drink wine, and she'd smile shyly and say 'I'd like that.' She was good at the shy smiles, Amy, always had been, in spite of being the least shy person I'd ever known.

There was nobody at home when I got back. Dad and Wilfred were still out. I was glad about that. I opened the door and went through to the kitchen and sat there for a bit. Just sat. I didn't cry and I didn't hear Mum singing, even though the house was empty. Perhaps if I'd been able to cry I would've heard her, or she would've heard me, but I couldn't. I just sat there at the kitchen table and all I felt was anger. At Amy, but mostly at myself.

How could I have been so stupid? How could I have let her persuade me to do it?

She probably planned it all along, said the voice in my head, the crocodile voice. When I'd shown her Jack's photograph she thought she'd have him for herself. Pretty little, funny little Amy May.

I don't know how long I sat there, but after a while I went upstairs and took off Dad's old clothes and shoved them back in his drawer and then I went and lay down on my bed wrapped up in the coverlet I'd had since I was little. I stayed there staring at the damp patch on the ceiling until I heard the front door open and the sound of Dad's boots and Wilfred's excited scrabbling and then Dad's voice calling, 'Lil? You here?' Then he must've seen my boots at the bottom of the stairs and thought that I'd gone to bed early because I had to get up for work the next day.

I never wrote to Jack again. When his letters arrived, I didn't open them, just shoved them into the biscuit tin under my bed with the others. *It's not me he wants*, I thought, *it's Amy. I saw that when they kissed. If she wants to write to him, let her. He won't want any more letters from me.*

That was a bad day, the day I dressed up as a boy and followed Jack and Amy round the zoo. But things were about to get an awful lot worse.

The next few days passed in a miserable blur. It was my last week of working day shifts at the Arsenal before going on to nights like Dad. I hadn't wanted to do it at first, but they gave you no choice, and now I was glad. I didn't want time to think. Amy had come round a couple of evenings after the day at the zoo. I knew it was her, I could tell her knock, but Dad was at work and I pretended I was out or asleep. The second time I found a note on the doormat when I got up in the morning. It said:

LILY DODD I KNOW YOU'RE THERE WHY ARE YOU IGNORING ME?

I screwed it up and threw it on the fire.

The days passed and she didn't come any more. I reckoned she must've gone back to France. She never wrote again, but then, as Dad said, she was never much of a one for writing letters. I told myself I didn't care. She wasn't the person I thought she was. Nobody would treat their best friend like that, trick them and then go off with their boy. She knew how I felt about Jack, I'd told her everything, just like I always did, and now I felt stupid. I felt stupid for telling her, stupid for going along with her plan, stupid for ever loving her and thinking she loved me.

I'd lie in bed at night going over and over it in my head, finding more things to blame her for, more reasons to hate her. The picture of her lifting up her face to kiss Jack would appear whenever I shut my eyes. I managed to convince myself that I was better off without her, I didn't care what happened to her in France, I didn't care if she never wrote to me, didn't care if I never saw her again. I had other friends! The girls in the team, the Rockets, they were much better friends to me than Amy May ever was.

And I'd lie there on my back staring at the

darkness, and when I finally turned over to try and sleep I'd find my pillow was damp with tears.

'Ohhhhhhh . . . !'

A huge groan went up in the women's canteen. The lights had gone out again.

It was the third time it had happened since I'd started working nights. The work was still boring and sometimes the nights seemed to go on for ever, but at least it meant I could walk in to work with Dad, and we could go home together, and then watch the sun coming up over the river when we took Wilfred out for his morning walk. Dad had been moved to the Danger Buildings, where he worked with explosives, like Jess and the other Canary Girls, and I was still in the New Fuse Factory. Working nights also meant I was away from Joe Crawford, because he was still on days, which was good. Ever since we'd beaten the Nippies, he'd hated me even more, if that was possible, finding any excuse to criticize me or report me to Miss Foxwell, fine me for being late or for having a bit of hair sticking out from under my cap. So I was glad to be away from him, though I wasn't glad about much else. I missed the friends I'd made on the day shift. Most of all I missed playing football during break.

Dinner time (as they called it) was at midnight on the night shift and there was nothing to do except sit in the women's canteen. I hadn't got to know any of the girls yet, so I usually sat on my own. I didn't mind that. I liked the factory at night. It still felt alive, its machines still hummed and clanked and sparked and the lights lit up the sky. There hadn't been an air raid for so long that they'd got careless with the shutters that were meant to cover the windows so the lights didn't show to the enemy aircraft. I'd just been out for a breath of air and had stood for a few minutes watching the river. There were hardly any boats at that time of night and it looked still and peaceful, rippling black and white in the moonlight. It was cold – Christmas had come and gone that year without anyone really noticing – and the night smelt of soot and chemicals and mud. There were no searchlights to break up the sky with their long white fingers that night. I didn't know why then, but I do now. They turned the searchlights off when they'd detected enemy aircraft making their way up the Thames estuary. It was so they wouldn't see us, and it was always too late.

I took one last look at the river and then turned to go into the canteen, where the warmth and light and noise hit me like a wall. There were girls at every table, laughing and eating and teasing each other, faces glowing in the light of the overhead lamps, all making the most of their free time before they had to get back to work. I sat down at the end of one of the tables on my own and started to unwrap my cheese sandwich, and that was when the lights went out.

It wasn't unusual, it happened sometimes. In a way it broke up the boredom. There were more giggles and a few comments in the dark:

'Not again!'

'Here we go!'

But the chatting and laughter died away into the darkness as we listened. There was no sound. The machines had stopped. The constant hum and clatter of the Arsenal's machines had been silenced and the factory was completely still. That was when girls started to grope for each other's hands and a voice from the other end of the room called out:

'No need to worry, girls! Probably just another false alarm!'

A murmur went around. This had happened before and the girls were brave, but it was so very very dark and the silence was so very very complete. Someone somewhere let out a single sob and was immediately shushed by someone else.

'We'll just have to sit it out, girls!' It was the same voice again, one of the lady overlookers who worked the night shifts. 'How about a sing-song? All together, now!' And she started to sing in a high quavery voice. 'Ten green bottles . . .'

Her voice made the silence seem deeper. A couple of girls started to join in, but their voices died away as we heard the hum of the aircraft overhead. The planes they sent now, the Giants, didn't seem as terrifying as the horrible great Zeppelins, but they could do just as much damage. More, if anything, because they weren't so easy for our guns to bring down. So we sat there, holding hands, in complete silence. It was as if we were afraid to make a noise in case they heard us, which was silly as we knew that the factory was lit up and that the silvery moonlit snake of the river would make it easy to see from the air.

Then – the scream of a bomb falling, a roar of engines, an explosion. The whole building shook. White faces looking at each other in the dark. *We're hit. The Arsenal is hit.* Nobody said a word. Some girls hugged each other and rocked silently but most of us just sat there, holding hands.

Then, a voice outside, a man: 'It's the Danger Buildings! All hands to the Danger Buildings!'

And the lady overlooker: 'Not us, girls! We stay here!'

The clang of a fire engine's bell sounded in the distance. We looked at each other and a murmur went around the room. The Danger Buildings, that's where they dealt with the chemicals, the poisons that made the girls' skin and hair turn yellow. The explosives. We all knew what it could mean if a fire started there. I knew what it meant most of all. Because that's where my dad was working.

I let go of the hand of the girl next to me, realizing her fingernails had dug into my palm. My hand was sticky with sweat.

'Sit tight, girls.' The voice of the overlooker again. 'Sit tight for now. There's nothing we can do.'

I got up. *There is something I can do*, I thought. *I can go and find my dad.*

'Sit down, girl!' she shouted. 'Where do you think you're going?'

I'm going to the door.

'Come back!'

Outside was chaos. Men running through the dark, coming at me from every direction, shouting instructions, the sound of fire engines, an ambulance, somewhere a horse gave a terrified whinny. *Which way are the Danger Buildings? Which way?*

I stood there, the men swirling round me, their feet pounding on the wooden boards and the moon shining down, calm and quiet, turning the scene black and white. Then the noise and the bustle seemed to fade away in the moonlight and I heard:

'She's my lady love, she is my dove, my baby love . . .'

It was Mum. And as I listened to her singing my song, a path seemed to clear in front of me, lit up by the moonlight. I followed it, slowly and carefully putting one foot in front of another, through the frantic men, past the end of the canteen, across the open ground, around the corner and there, there was the building the bomb had hit, half the roof gone, a wall caved in, a door hanging off its hinges. There were clouds of smoke – or was it just dust? – rising off it, pale in the moonlight.

'Get away from there, love! It's been hit. We think the bomb's still live! The whole place could go up any time.'

I went inside, stepping carefully over the rubble around the door. Mum's voice was louder here.

'She's no girl for sitting down to dream . . .'

It was pitch black inside with rubble everywhere, but I stepped over it easily without looking.

'She's the only queen Laguna knows . . .'

Then, the sound of a groan in the darkness. Someone called out, 'Over here!' but it wasn't Dad, so I stepped over him. Through a doorway into a side room, moonlight streaming through a broken shutter, and there he was.

'Dad.'

A beam from the roof was lying across him, which I lifted up easily. His face was white and his eyes open. And there was blood, blood on his face. The world seemed to turn inside out and I thought, *This is what it feels like when your father dies.*

I knelt down beside him. I didn't know what else to do. And then his eyes moved in his face and he saw me. And he smiled. He actually smiled.

'Lily-oh.'

Dad.

I stroked the hair off his forehead and buried my face in his chest, breathing in his familiar smell of tobacco and engine oil, and the whole of the last few weeks faded into nothingness. The game against the Nippies and Crawford cheating, Jack and Amy kissing and me dressed up as a boy, spying on them from behind a pillar. The crocodile with his evil smile. All the hurt and anger and stupidness just melted away into the moonlight.

'I'm sorry, Dad,' I whispered.

He smiled again. He didn't look hurt, just tired. 'Nothing to be sorry for, Lil,' he said. 'Just don't give up on me, eh? Don't ever give up. Fighting. Football. Don't ever give up being my Lily of Laguna.'

'Never, Dad,' I said and I kissed his cheek. 'I promise.'

'My Lily,' he whispered, his eyes closing. 'And. My rose . . .'

I looked at him. He was quite still. *Dad?* said the voice in my head. Then, out loud: 'Dad!'

And I started to shout.

'Help! Help needed here! Someone, please! Help!'

PART THREE
Autumn 1918

They'd taken Dad to the hospital, loaded carefully on to a stretcher. I went with him, sitting in the back of the ambulance as it rattled and rocked through the night-time streets, holding his hand while a voice in my head chanted in time with the rhythm of the wheels, *Don't be dead, don't be dead, please please please please, please don't be dead* . . .

And then in the hospital, sitting by his bed, the blood cleaned off his face, a bandage around his head and a clean white sheet pulled up to his chin, his eyes still closed, the doctor examining him, saying he'd had a nasty blow to the head, but there didn't seem to be too much damage done. They'd know more when he came round, the doctor said.

And then, in the morning, Dad came round and opened his eyes and . . . he couldn't see. The nasty blow to his head had damaged his brain, the doctor said. It was unlikely he'd ever be able to see again.

He was blind.

Dad didn't say anything at first when the doctor gave us the news. He just shifted in his bed as if he was a bit uncomfortable, and reached for my hand. I took it in both of mine. It felt cool and dry and rough with work. I could feel the line of calluses across the palm. He even smiled a bit as he turned his face towards me and said, 'We'll cope, won't we, Lily-oh?'

I tried to reply, I tried to say something, but the words got stuck in my throat and I was glad when a voice interrupted.

'Lil?' I looked up to see Billy Cracken standing by the bed. There were beads of sweat on his forehead, and he was breathing fast as if he'd been running. He smelt of the outdoors, of woodsmoke and hay and horses. 'They told me at the factory,' he said. 'I heard.'

'Is that Bill Cracken?' said Dad. 'Nice of you to

come, boy. How are you?'

Billy looked at him, and then at me, and he knew. He sat down on the bed and tried to smile. I swallowed down the feelings that were rising up in my throat.

'I'm fine, sir,' said Bill. His outline went all blurry as I looked at him, and I had to take a very deep breath so as not to cry.

'And the horses?'

'They're fine too.'

'Good, good,' said Dad. 'Good.' And then he gave a little smile and nodded in my direction. 'No football for me for a while, I'm afraid, Bill,' he said. 'I was just saying to Lil here, wasn't I, Lil?' I nodded, forgetting he couldn't see me. 'That we'll cope. Isn't that right, Lily-oh?'

This time I found I could reply. I blinked my eyes slowly, then squeezed his hand and bent over and kissed his forehead.

''Course we will, Dad,' I said. 'We always do, don't we?'

And we did cope, for a while. Dad couldn't go back to work, of course, so we were dependent on my wages to pay the rent and buy food. But that was fine. Even though I'd had to get permission to go back to working days after the accident, I was still earning enough to keep us both. I was proud of that, and it meant I could play football again in the dinner break. When I went to work, Dad stayed at home, learning to find his way around the house on his own and even teaching himself to do little jobs. He got hold of a white stick and, with the help of Stan-next-door, started taking Wilfred out for walks around Woolwich and on the marshes. He even talked about starting football training with the Rockets once the summer was over.

'We'll get some more matches organized next season,' he said. 'Join a proper league.'

And we used to talk, me and Dad, late into the night at the kitchen table, drinking tea and making plans for the Rockets. We didn't see much of Billy, he was too busy with his horses, but Jess would come round sometimes with fish and chips and we'd talk about the ladies' teams up north we'd heard about, from places like Preston and St Helens, how good they were (it was rumoured they'd even beaten men's teams) and Jess would say, 'But none of them have got a keeper like ours, Mr

Dodd,' and Dad would nod and smile and I'd shake my head and pretend to deny it, but deep down, deep deep down, I knew it was true.

And then everything changed again.

I was at work when the guns sounded over London. We all knew it was going to happen, but when it did, at eleven o'clock on that November morning, we all just stopped whatever we were doing, put down our tools and stared at each other. Nobody cheered, nobody danced, nobody hugged or kissed or cried. We just stood there, not quite letting ourselves believe it.

The war was over.

After the sound of the guns had died away there was a moment's silence and then slowly, gradually, came a faint sound from outside the factory. It started as a sort of hum, like a distant swarm of bees, that got louder and louder until it was all around us and I realized what it was. It was the sound of people, cheering. All over London, people had stopped what they were doing and were cheering the end of the war. There were other sounds too: sirens from the boats on the river, hoots from buses and trams in the street and then the Arsenal's own hooters sending joyful blasts of sound into the sky, and then finally came the bells, the clash of church bells, ringing out all over London. The air was full of joy and clatter.

And still we just stood there, lost in our own thoughts.

What would happen to us, the girls who had kept the soldiers at the front supplied with their bombs and bullets? We were glad the war was over, of course we were, glad no more men would lose their lives or their legs or their eyesight. Glad no more women would lose their sons and husbands, no more children would lose their dads. No more girls would lose their brothers and their sweethearts.

But we would lose our jobs. Dad and I would both be out of work. And what would happen to the Rockets? Would they let us play on the men's grounds when the soldiers came back?

'Lil!'

Jess had arrived next to me, her face cut in half by the biggest grin I'd seen since she scored the winning goal against the Nippies. Around her, the whole workshop was bursting into life as the girls blinked and looked around them as if they were waking up out of a dream. A whisper started going around, moving from work bench to work bench as the news sank in.

'Can it be true?'

'Can it really be true?'

'After all this time?'

'It must be. Just listen. Listen to the bells.'

And we all stopped and listened, and the bells were clanging, and, as we all started to believe it, the whispers turned to chatter as the girls started to hug each other and laugh with delight. Two of them even linked arms and started to dance, while others kept time for them by clicking their fingers and clapping their hands.

It was true. The news finally sank in that the war was over, and the whole of the Woolwich Arsenal erupted into joy.

'They've given us the day off!' Jess shouted above the noise. 'So we're all heading into town. Come on!'

She grabbed my arm and pulled me outside. People were emerging from their workshops all over the factory, blinking in the daylight and looking round at the grey November day as if they'd woken up from a dream. Everything looked exactly the same: the sooty brick walls, the drifts of fog that wrapped themselves round the base of the buildings and lingered in hollows in the marshy ground, but it all felt different. It was as if the world had suddenly turned from grey into full colour. Jess and I and the other Rockets grabbed our coats and bags and joined the stream of laughing, chattering, dancing girls heading out of the factory gates.

'Here you are, dearies, roses all round!'

Out in the square, a flag seller had appeared from nowhere and the old lady on the flower stall was handing out flowers to anyone who wanted them. Mr Singh was giving away lengths of ribbon in yellow and green and scarlet. We lingered long enough to stick flowers in our hair and tie ribbons around each other's wrists and waists and heads and be thoroughly kissed and swept off our feet by some Australian soldiers, before Jess made us all hold hands and pulled us towards the river where we clattered, laughing and screaming, down the steps into the foot tunnel. Then out the other end, where we squeezed on to a tram and somehow ended up at Trafalgar Square, where, along with thousands and thousands of other people, we danced and cheered and sang and shouted for the King.

It seemed like nobody in London stayed indoors that day. Everybody was out on the streets, waving flags, dancing and singing, shaking each other's hands, kissing random strangers. There were people everywhere. Boys letting off fireworks, men in uniform, nurses, some pushing their patients in wheelchairs. There were men in pyjamas and on crutches, as if all the hospitals had opened their doors and let the injured out to celebrate along with the rest of the city. I saw a man spinning round on one crutch, and another in a dressing gown sweeping a respectable-looking lady up into his arms and kissing her on both cheeks before setting her gently on to an empty plinth in the corner of the square.

Somehow, in the course of that mad day when I'd danced and laughed and kissed and hugged more people than I'd ever met in my life, I got separated from Jess and the others. A military band was playing 'It's a Long Way to Tipperary' (how many times did I hear that tune?) and everyone was singing along, bellowing at the tops of their voices. When the song came to an end, there was a little pause before the band started up again. It was a different tune this time, a sad, slow one that Dad used to sing sometimes.

'*Keep the home fires burning, while my heart is yearning . . .*'

Nobody sang along this time. The crowd fell completely silent and a woman next to me who'd been singing as loud as anyone else, suddenly started to cry. I touched her arm, not knowing what else to do and she turned a tear-stained face to me. She was quite old, in her forties perhaps, and she stared at me, not bothering to wipe her eyes or hide her tears.

'How can I be happy,' she said, 'when I lost my man two weeks ago?'

I didn't know what to say, so I didn't say anything. Her face suddenly crumpled.

'He's never coming home, is he?' She sounded almost angry and grabbed my arm so hard it hurt.

'Is he?' Her face looked ugly and wet and red as she clutched my arm through my coat.

I shook my head. 'No,' I said, looking at the pavement because I couldn't bear to look at her. 'No. I don't suppose he is.'

She gave a cold little laugh and released my arm. 'It's not over, is it?' she said. 'Not for me, not for any of us. Nothing will ever be the same again.'

You're right, I thought. *It won't be the same for any of us.* My dad had lost his eyesight, I'd lost my best friend and my boy, and soon I'd lose my job and probably my football team as well. The band was playing something cheerful again now and people were swirling around me, singing and dancing and laughing and kissing each other like they were before but I felt cold inside. I had nothing to do with any of these people. Nothing.

'No,' I said to the woman again. 'Everything's different now.'

She shook her head. 'I'm best out of here,' she said, then turned and walked away.

I watched her small hunched figure making its way through the crowds of red-faced, grinning people until I couldn't see it any more. I felt sick.

I'm best out of here too, I thought, and turned my back on the square and started to walk. I didn't know where I was going, I just wanted to be away from the noise and madness, so I headed towards some trees a short way off and found myself in a park. It was quieter there. There were a few couples, wrapped up in each other, sitting on benches or lying on the man's khaki greatcoat spread out on the grass. They weren't saying much, or doing much, most of them, just looking at each other, the men in uniform, the girls smiling at them, often through tears. It was beginning to get dark now and starting to drizzle. I walked along a path past a lake that contained nothing but mud, and wondered what I was going to do.

And then I heard a voice: 'Lil? Is that you?'

It was Billy Cracken, sitting on his own on a bench facing the mud-filled lake. He had a string of bunting round his neck, a football beside him and a duck at his feet. Like me he must've got fed up with the crowds.

'Bill.'

I wasn't surprised to see him; everyone was in the centre of town that day. He looked older than I remembered, and there was the faint shadow of a moustache on his upper lip I hadn't noticed before. I sat down on the bench next to him and for a moment we sat in silence, watching the speckled brown duck as it padded around on its flat greenish feet, pulling crossly at bits of straggly grass. I was so happy to see Billy that my throat felt tight and my eyes prickled with stupid tears. It was the duck that spoke first.

'Quack,' it said, and glared at us with its beady black eyes.

We laughed, and Bill gave it a crust of bread from a paper bag on his lap. 'I've always liked ducks,' he said.

'Me too,' I said. For a moment we both watched the duck gobble grumpily at the bread and then look to Bill for more. 'No matter how bad things get,' I said, 'there'll always be ducks in the world.'

He nodded and emptied the last of the crumbs on to the grass. 'Are things bad, Lil?' he said, without looking at me.

I nodded. 'Pretty bad,' I said.

And then I told him. I told him about Jack and Amy, and how I'd followed them to the zoo dressed up in my dad's clothes, and then seen them kiss so I'd stopped writing to Jack and shoved all his letters under my bed without opening them. Then I told him about how worried I was because now I was going to lose my job at the Arsenal, and then what would happen to me and Dad and the Rockets? How would we survive if I couldn't work? How could I survive without football?

Bill didn't say anything for such a long time that I thought he'd stopped listening, but then he said, 'I've got an idea.'

I looked at him, a question in my eyes. The duck had given up on getting any more bread, and was stomping away towards the mud-filled lake. I didn't hold out much hope that my problems could all be solved by Billy Cracken, but I was curious to know about his idea. He still didn't speak, just watched the duck as it plopped into a little muddy pool at the edge of the lake.

'What is it then, Bill? Your idea. Tell us.'

Bill looked at me and for the first time that day gave me a proper grin. The gap between his front teeth made him look younger than he was and reminded me of the boy I used to play football with at school.

'All in good time, Lil. But first,' he got up from the bench and picked up his football, 'how about a game?'

CHAPTER EIGHTEEN

'*That's* your idea?'

We were back on the bench, warm and breathless from our game, and I was staring at Billy Cracken in disbelief. His spiky brown hair was beaded all over with tiny drops of drizzle and across the park the people outside Buckingham Palace were shouting for the King.

'*We want the King . . . we want the King . . .*'

Bill grinned and ran his hand over his hair, scattering the drops of water as a huge roar went up from the crowd. The King and Queen must've appeared on the palace balcony. 'That,' he said, wiping his hand on his trousers, 'is my idea.'

He'd told me that he was going for a trial with a proper football club. Tottenham Hotspur. He knew he didn't have much hope of getting in: though he loved football and had a really good eye, he didn't have what it took to make it as a professional. He was too skinny for one thing, and too gentle, and though he was quick and good at distributing the ball from his favourite position at centre-half, he was too easily knocked off the ball by players who were bigger and stronger than him.

He must have guessed what I was thinking. 'I know I don't have much chance,' he said. 'But I'll kick myself if I don't give it a go. And so will you, Lily Dodd.'

'You think I should do a trial. For a men's team.'

'Why not?'

And I repeated what Amy May had said to me all that time ago on Plumstead Marshes.

'Because, Billy Cracken, in case you hadn't noticed, I am a girl.'

'So what? You're as good as any man. Better than most.'

I didn't know what to say to that, so I just said, 'Are you mad?'

Bill looked around as if I was talking to

someone else. 'Not since I last checked. Think about it, Lil, it'd solve all your problems. You'd bring in a wage, a good one too, doing something you love. How else are you going to pay the rent if you lose your job at the Arsenal?'

'I suppose I'll have to go into service. Get a job as a maid.'

'You'd hate that.'

'I know.'

'And you'd be rotten at it.'

'True.'

'*And* it would mean you'd have to leave home, likely as not. Then who would look after your dad?'

'I know, I know, I know. But – go for a trial with a men's team? I couldn't do it, Bill.' I sounded very certain, but as I said it I felt a little flicker of something at the back of my brain. I looked at him. 'Could I?'

'You did it before, disguised yourself as a boy. You just said. Got away with it too.'

'I wasn't playing football, though, was I? I was just sneaking round London spying on my friend. And I'm not sure I did get away with it, actually.'

'Did anybody say anything to you when you were out?'

'No, but—'

'No shouts, no rude comments, no chiacking?'

'Not that I noticed. And a guard at the station called me "son".'

'There you go. This is London, Lil. If someone spots a girl walking round the streets dressed up as a man, d'you really think they're going to keep their mouths shut? I wouldn't. If you tried it round our way half the kids would be following you around shouting things and the other half'd be throwing stones.'

I laughed. 'You're right there.'

'I know I am. Face it, Lil, if someone had spotted you, you'd've had a trail of boys following you from Woolwich to Regent's Park.'

'Yes, but it's one thing to walk across London dressed as a boy without being spotted. It's another to play football in a men's team.'

'You'll regret if you don't. Admit it – now I've given you the idea, you'll regret it for the rest of your life if you don't give it a try.'

Bill got up suddenly and picked up his football

from the bench beside him. 'Come on,' he said and turned to go, bouncing the ball on the ground, then dribbling it in front of him.

'Where are we going?'

'Home. Back to Woolwich. To find you some kit.'

'But, Bill . . .'

He stopped, the heavy football balanced on the end of his foot for a second, before he flicked it up and caught it in between his hands then turned to look at me. Outside the palace the crowd was singing 'God Save the King'. 'What?' he said. I could tell he was getting impatient with my objections. 'What is it now?'

'Say I do get in. Through the trial, I mean. Say they offer me a place in the team.'

'Yes?'

'What about the changing rooms? Hey? You didn't think of that, did you?'

He shrugged. 'You'll think of something. Tell them you're shy. Religious. I don't know.'

'And the baths afterwards?'

'You've got a nasty rash.' He turned to go again.

'Bill!'

This time he stopped without turning round.

Even his back looked annoyed. He said nothing, so I spoke:

'What about my hair?'

We cut it off. I found an old pair of sewing scissors that must have belonged to my mum, and Billy sawed through the great long plait that had hung down my back for as long as I could remember, the plait that used to get pulled by boys several times a day at school, and wound itself around my neck like a snake when I was in bed at night so I used to dream I was being strangled.

My lovely hair, Jess had called it. She'd said I had lovely hair.

Well, I didn't any more. Because Billy Cracken cut it off.

We'd found the house empty when we got back – Dad and Wilfred must've gone out with Stan-next-door to join in the celebrations in Beresford Square – so we went up to my room. I sorted out the clothes I'd worn on that awful day at the zoo, and Billy had picked up some of his own football kit for me to try.

I was standing in front of the mirror, staring at

my reflection. Bill had said I couldn't wear my own kit, the one I wore with the Rockets, because it looked wrong for a man, so I was wearing a pair of my dad's old football shorts, held up round the waist by a bit of string. I also had a football jersey of Bill's, which smelt of woodsmoke and horses and was a bit too short in the arms, and a pair of his old socks which had holes in both feet. In my hand was the heavy rope of dark red hair that Bill had just chopped off.

I ruffled what remained of the hair on my head. It stood up, fluffy and a bit wavy, curling round my face. I turned to Bill. My head felt light and strange without the weight of my plait.

'What d'you reckon, Bill?' I said. 'Will I do?'

'Not sure.' Bill was sitting on the bed. He got up and stood next to me, looking at my reflection. We looked funny standing there side by side in the mirror, even though he was nearly as tall as me now. For the first time I thought, *I haven't asked him about himself. How he's been since Dad's accident, what he's been doing. Is he still living at the children's home, working with the horses at Woolwich Barracks? What will happen to his job now the war's over?* All this was running through my head, and then . . . *he looks tired*, I thought. *I hope he's all right*. But before I could say any of this, Bill was speaking again.

'You need something else.' He took a step back and looked me up and down. 'To be totally convincing. A neckerchief, perhaps? I know!' He stopped, looking at my face in the mirror with his head on one side. 'D'you think you could grow a moustache, Lil? That'd make all the difference.'

'What?' I turned to look at him. His mouth twitched, and I remembered all the times he'd made me laugh at school. 'Hm,' I said, turning back to my reflection. 'Perhaps if I concentrated really, really hard.' And I screwed up my face to show him what I meant.

We grinned at each other in the glass and I remembered why I'd always liked this boy so much. It wasn't just that he was the one who first got me playing football with the boys, back when we were seven years old. He always seemed to know when I was feeling miserable or scared and would say something daft to make me laugh and make everything feel ordinary again.

'One thing's for sure,' I said, 'I could probably grow a moustache before you do, Billy Cracken!'

'True.' Bill touched the few soft hairs on his upper lip. 'I'm just not the sort, I s'pose. Not your hairy type of bloke.'

'Neither' – I slapped his arm – 'am I! Or perhaps you didn't notice!'

'Owwww!' Bill said in a little-girly voice, clutching his arm. 'Nasty!' Then he looked at himself in the mirror standing next to me and spoke in his normal voice. 'Just because I can't grow a moustache, doesn't mean I'm not all man, mind.' He struck a pose, flexing his arms like a strongman. 'Grrrrr! I'll get you! I could beat you to a pulp, me!'

'Idiot!' I pushed him and he fell back on the bed, while I turned back to the mirror. I hung the plait over my mouth, scrunching my top lip up to my nose to keep it in place, then turned to Bill. 'What d'you reckon? Does it suit me?' It was hard keeping it in place while I talked.

'Not bad.' Bill got to his feet and looked at me, taking the plait of hair away from my face. His eyes were serious. 'Actually, Lil, you don't need a moustache. You look perfect. Like . . .' He swallowed and looked away. 'Like the most prettiest boy ever.'

Pretty! Nobody had ever called me that before. I looked at the floor, unable to look at either Bill or my reflection. My cheeks were burning.

Bill must've felt embarrassed too, because he gave a funny little laugh and added, 'Just as well your dad won't be able to see you, eh?'

'Bill!' I stared at him for a second, mouth open, not believing what he'd just said. 'That is a terrible thing to say!' I grabbed my plait from him and started to whip him with it. 'You're an awful person! Awful!'

'Argh!' He fell back on the bed, laughing, then when I carried on whipping him, curled up into a ball. 'Stop it, Lil! I'm sorry! Stop! Sto-o-op—'

And then we froze. We'd both heard it. The front door opening, footsteps in the hall, the dog scrabbling and barking, and then Dad's voice:

'Lily? Is that you? What's going on up there? LILY!'

CHAPTER NINETEEN

The plait fell from my hand as Bill and I looked at each other. I felt cold all over, so cold I couldn't move. I opened my mouth but the fear had got into my throat and no words would come out.

What were we going to do? I'd never had a boy round to the house before, not while Dad was out, and certainly not in my bedroom. What must Dad have thought when he walked in the front door and heard us, shrieking and laughing and thumping about upstairs?

What must he be thinking now?

Bill started to move, very slowly and carefully, unfolding his body and getting up off the bed without making a sound. Dad's voice came again, this time from the bottom of the stairs. He didn't sound angry, just surprised, which was somehow worse.

'Lil? Have you got someone up there with you?'

Bill moved close to me, so close I could feel his breath on my neck. 'You're going to have to tell him,' he said very quietly.

I nodded, once, twice, three times. Then I took a deep breath, pulled back my shoulders and stuck my chin in the air in what Amy used to call my Duchess of Pilkington pose, and, as if I was walking out to my goal before a match, I marched over to the door and flung it open.

'Yes, Dad!' I called. 'Billy Cracken's here! And we've got something very important to tell you!'

There was a shocked silence and then, from behind me, a sudden snort. I turned round to see Bill doubled up with silent, helpless laughter.

'What?' I said. '*What?*'

Dad took it surprisingly well, all things considered. I think he was so relieved when I didn't announce Billy Cracken and I were planning to get married that nothing else could upset him. He sat very upright at the kitchen table, with the little dog at his feet and his eyes moving between me and Bill as each of us spoke. We stood there in front of him, like two naughty children who'd been caught doing something we shouldn't, which I suppose was true in a way.

I don't know how I expected Dad to react when we'd finished explaining our plan. Perhaps he'd say we were mad, they'd spot straight away that I was a girl. And even if I did get through the trial, I'd never be able to play with men. I'd get hurt. I'd never get away with it. It wasn't decent. *And what about the changing rooms?* (I was still really worried about that.)

I should've known better. My dad wasn't going to say any of that. The dad who'd always said, *Whatever you want to do, Lily, people will try and stop you. They'll tell you it's too hard, you won't like it, you'll be no good at it. But you must not let them, Lily-oh. You Must Not Let Them.*

So he didn't say any of that. He didn't say anything at all, actually. Not at first. After I'd finished explaining how I was going to disguise myself as a boy and go for a place in a men's team, and Bill had told him that the trials were next Sunday up at the Spurs' training ground in north London, Dad took a long, deep breath, then looked up to where we were standing and said, 'Spurs, eh? Ah well, nobody's perfect.' Then, while Bill and I stood there with our mouths open, not knowing what to say, Dad laughed and pushed himself up out of his chair. 'Come here, Lily-oh,' he said. 'Let's see what this new hairdo of yours is like.'

That's when I knew everything was going to be all right. I went over and knelt down on the floor, putting my arms round Dad's legs while he felt my hair with both hands, nodding to himself in a satisfied way, and then he said: 'Next Sunday, did you say, Bill?'

'Yes, Mr Dodd.'

'That's less than a week away. We'd best get down that park and do some training.'

It was still dark when I woke up next Sunday. I lay in bed, staring at the ceiling and listening to Dad downstairs talking to Wilfred and feeling my heart thudding in my chest. Perhaps I was ill, I thought, so ill that I wouldn't be able to go to the trial. Even

Billy Cracken would accept that. But then I felt my forehead with my hand and I knew I wasn't ill. I was just scared.

I got up slowly, very slowly, and went over to the window. It was just beginning to get light, and the whole of London was wrapped up in a cold grey mist. The sky hung low over the rooftops.

'Morning, Lil!' Dad must have heard me moving about upstairs. 'Think you can manage an egg?' he called. 'Stan brought some round yesterday, but you might have to cook it yourself.'

'No, thanks, Dad.' My voice sounded surprisingly normal. 'Just a cup of tea will do me.' I turned to the mirror. 'This is it, Lily Dodd,' I said to my reflection. 'There's no going back now.' A deep breath, and I pulled my nightdress off over my head and stood there for a second shivering with cold and fear.

Time to get ready.

I'd bought a wide roll of stretchy bandage from the chemist and I wrapped that tightly round my chest, winding it round several times. I didn't have much to cover up, to be honest, but I wasn't taking any chances. Then, when I'd checked my side view several times in the mirror, and was happy with it, I got dressed. First, Dad's old shorts (I'd mended the tear in the back); then, over my bandaged chest, Bill's football jersey (which I'd washed in the kitchen sink so it didn't smell of him any more); and finally, I put on the red-and-white stripy socks that Jess's mum had knitted for all the Rockets, and pulled the matching knitted bobble hat over my cropped hair.

I was done. And yes, I looked like a footballer.

Over my kit I put the clothes I'd worn on that other Sunday, when I'd followed Amy to the zoo and seen her kiss my boy. Dad's old trousers, collarless shirt, jacket, my own boots. Then I stuffed the knitted hat into my pocket and pulled my dad's second-best cap over my eyes. I nodded to myself in the mirror and touched a finger to the cap in a little salute.

'Good luck, mate,' I said and winked. The boy in the mirror winked back, then turned and left the room.

Slowly, very slowly, we made our way down the stairs, the boy and me, and by the time we got to the bottom we were one person again. Dad was standing there, holding on to the banister with one hand. In the other he had the football boots that had once been his and were now mine, gleaming like fresh conkers as always. Somehow he'd managed to polish them.

'You didn't have to do that, Dad.'

'Oh, but I did. Can't have my girl going out in dirty boots, can I?'

'I'm not a girl now, Dad. Remember?' I took the boots from him and he smiled, his eyes looking at me but seeing nothing.

'So who are you, Lil?' he said, suddenly serious.

'What d'you mean?' His question gave me a strange, empty feeling, as if the world had suddenly shifted and everything looked the same but was somehow different. I was still Lily Dodd, wasn't I? I certainly felt the same inside. I was the same small scared person who loved football and dogs and Dad, and used to laugh with her best friend and write letters to a boy at the front. It was just my outside that was different. Wasn't it?

'Well, you can hardly be Lily, can you?' Dad was saying. 'Not now you're a boy. What's your name?'

I stared at him. Of course. That was one thing

Bill and I hadn't considered.

Dad grinned. 'Don't tell me you haven't thought of one.'

My mind was a total blank. 'I don't know, Dad. What do you reckon? I'm too nervous to think.'

'Hm. Let's see.' Dad closed his eyes and reached up and traced the outline of my face with his forefinger. Then: 'Charlie,' he said. 'You seem like a Charlie to me.'

And so, from that moment on, I was Charlie. Charlie Dodd. I liked the sound of it.

'Charlie?' said Bill. 'Why Charlie?'

We were sitting on the train going up to the Spurs' ground at White Hart Lane. We'd arranged to meet at the station and he'd walked past me three times without recognizing me, which made me very happy. When he'd walked past me the fourth time I'd reached out and pinched his bum, and he'd turned to glare at me with such a look of shock and outrage that I'd stopped pretending and started to laugh. I felt better after that. If I could fool Bill Cracken then perhaps, just perhaps, I could fool the blokes at Spurs. I looked across at him on the opposite seat.

'What's wrong with Charlie?' I said. A little girl across the aisle looked up at the sound of my voice. 'It's a good name,' I said, more quietly. 'Dad chose it.'

Bill said nothing, and for a few moments we just sat and watched the grey houses flick past the window. Then he nodded, almost to himself.

'Charlie Dodd,' he said. 'Yup, it works. I like it. I like it a lot.'

'Charlie Dodd, sir.' This time I remembered to lower the pitch of my voice as I gave my name to the man at the desk. 'Goalkeeper.'

The man looked up from his notebook. Bill had already given him his name, and I could feel my heart thudding in my chest as the man's eyes travelled over me, taking in my shabby jacket and trousers, the cap pulled down over my hair.

'Goalkeeper, eh?' He pulled at his moustache thoughtfully. 'Well, you've certainly got the height for it, son. Any good?'

'I like to think so, sir,' I said. 'I've been with the Woolwich works' team for the duration.' Then, feeling more confident, I tried a little joke. 'Not much gets past me, sir.'

'Hm.' He looked at me over his glasses. 'Not much gets past me either, Dodd, so watch your step. Get too big for your boots here, we'll slap you right back down.'

'Yes, sir,' I said. 'Sorry, sir.'

He made another note in his book, then closed it with a snap, got to his feet and clapped his hands for attention.

'Right, lads!' he said. 'Let's be having you!'

There were about eight or nine there for the trial apart from me and Bill, mostly boys of around our age or a bit older. Too old for school, too young for the trenches. They were standing around nervously, in ones and twos, clutching their kit bags and waiting to be told what to do. I was the only keeper, I reckoned – none of the others looked tall enough. Outside on the pitch I could hear some players kicking a ball about and calling to each other.

'Changing rooms are thattaway.' The man pointed to a door in the corner of the room, and I suddenly felt very glad I was wearing my kit under my clothes. 'So get into your kit, get out on that pitch and show us what you're made of!'

As the others shuffled off towards the door, I felt a hand on my elbow.

'Come on, Charlie,' said Bill. 'You heard the man. Let's get out on that pitch and show them what you're made of.'

Dad was sitting in the kitchen when I got in that night. Stan-next-door must've been round, because there was the remains of a fish supper on the table and Wilf was sniffing around for scraps on the floor. They both looked up as they heard the door, and Dad got halfway out of his seat.

'Well?' he said.

I stood in the doorway, my football boots slung over my shoulder, making the moment stretch as long as I could. Dad's face dropped when I didn't reply, and he sank back into his chair.

'Never mind, love,' he said. 'You gave it your best shot, and for that I'm proud of you. Come and have a cup of tea.' He stretched out his hand to find the teapot. Still, I said nothing. He felt for the other chair and patted the seat. 'Don't be glum, chum,' he said. I smiled. That was what he always used to say when I'd had a bad day at school. 'We'll manage somehow.'

I couldn't keep my mouth shut a moment longer. 'I'm sure we will, Dad,' I said, still taking my time. I hung my boots on the back of the door and went to sit down next to him. 'Three quid a week should be enough for us both, I reckon. After we've paid the rent that should leave – ooh, getting on for two quid for everything else?'

Dad froze, his hand on the edge of the table. He stayed there for a moment like a statue, then – very slowly and carefully, as if my news was a timid animal he didn't want to scare away – he turned his face towards me.

'Lily Dodd,' he said, 'are you telling me—'

'YES!' I yelled, then jumped to my feet and grabbed both his hands. 'Your daughter is Tottenham Hotspurs' new goalkeeper!'

CHAPTER TWENTY

I was a proper footballer, in a proper team.

A men's team!

And I was earning three pounds a week, more than I'd got working at the Arsenal and much more than I'd ever get working as a servant in someone's house.

I felt bad for Bill, of course I did. After the man with the moustache (who turned out to be Mr Grimshaw, the Spurs' manager) told me that he was going to offer me a contract, I left his office in a daze, not really knowing where I was going. I wandered out of the clubhouse and found Bill in the street, leaning against a wall waiting for me. I could tell by the way he was standing that he hadn't got in.

'Bill,' I said.

He looked up, a question in his eyes. I didn't say anything, just nodded, fighting to keep the grin off my face. I couldn't fight it for long, though, because just as I knew he hadn't got in, Bill knew that I had. His face broke into a grin so wide that it seemed to split his face in half.

'Yes?' he said.

I nodded again. 'Yes,' I said and bit my lip. I was dangerously close to tears, I don't know why.

Bill let out a huge whoop of joy, then grabbed me round the waist and tried to swing me round like he used to when we were in the playground and our team had won, but I was too big for that now. We used to be the same size, me and Bill, but when we were about ten I started to shoot up and outgrew him so fast that for a while he only came up to my shoulder, even though he was nearly as tall as me again now. When he found he couldn't swing me round, Bill grabbed my hand and started to waltz me down the pavement, singing at the top of his voice.

'I know she likes me, I know she likes me, because she says so . . .'

'Bill! Stop it! Let me go!' I was half laughing, half crying. Then I gave up and joined in and we both yelled:

'*She is my Lily of Laguna, she is my Lily and my rose . . .*'

Goodness knows what people thought as we danced around them, two boys dancing together, stumbling over each other's feet, laughing like idiots. Old ladies tutted and old men said 'Oi! Look where you're going!' and by the time we got to the station we were being followed by three little boys, two dogs and a man who'd just come out of the pub and wanted to join in. A policeman by the station entrance stared at us and looked as if he was about to say something, but we were both too happy to care.

'I knew you'd do it, Lil,' said Bill when we'd collapsed in the train and were sitting staring at each other, breathless and amazed. 'I knew it!'

'Charlie,' I said, looking round to make sure nobody had heard.

'Charlie.' He corrected himself, then instantly forgot. 'Oh, Lil. Whatever is your dad going to say? He's going to be so proud!'

I smiled, picturing Dad's face when I told him the news. And then I stopped smiling as another thought dropped into my brain. 'I wish he could see me,' I said. 'You know, when I play my first game.'

'Yes,' said Bill. 'Me too.'

We both looked out of the window for a bit, our thoughts flicking past with the houses. Then Bill said, 'When is it, then? The first game? Did they tell you?'

'Soon,' I said. 'Next week. Just a friendly. Clapton Orient.'

We looked at each other and chanted, 'No such thing as a friendly!' It was one of Dad's favourite sayings.

'We're just playing friendlies till the league starts up again properly,' I said when we'd stopped laughing.

'A lot of the players must still be in France, waiting to be demobilized.'

I nodded, thinking of Jack Darling and wondering what had happened to him. 'The ones that made it,' I said.

Bill nodded and we sat in silence again for a

few minutes.

'What about the old keeper?' Bill said, breaking the silence. 'Is he in France?'

'No, here. Works in munitions, never joined up.'

'So you're reserve?'

I nodded. 'I'll be on the bench for most of the first game,' I said. 'But Mr Grimshaw said he'd try and give me a few minutes towards the end.'

'And . . . is it all right if I come along? To watch, you know.'

I stared at him.

'I'd understand if you didn't want me to,' he said. 'If you feel a bit funny about it. Lil?' he said when I still didn't reply. 'Would that be all right?'

'Of course it's all right,' I said. 'Idiot! It was you who got me here, wasn't it? And anyway, how's my dad going to get halfway across London on his own?'

They'd already started laying off girls from the Arsenal as the men came drifting back from the front, so when I handed in my notice they accepted it straight away. Miss Barker knew what had happened to Dad, and asked me what I planned to do instead.

'I'm not quite sure, miss,' I said, cheerfully. 'I expect something will turn up.' I was getting better at lying, I thought, though I'd never be as good as Amy May.

Miss Barker gave me a look from behind her glasses and then said, 'Very well, Lily.' I could tell she didn't believe me. 'Let me know if you need a reference.'

'Yes, miss,' I said. 'Thank you, miss.'

I felt her eyes on my back as I skipped out of her office. No more long days and nights, no more filth and noise and boredom, no more standing in front of a machine doing the same thing hour after hour, until you were so tired and bored that you could barely stand up.

'Lil?'

It was Jess. I hadn't told her what had happened, hadn't told her I was leaving. I didn't know why, not really. Perhaps I thought I'd jinx it, my new life, if anybody else knew. I'd even pulled a hat over my short hair in case anyone asked me about it. It had to be a secret, all of it, between me and Dad and Billy Cracken.

'What are you doing here?' she said. 'Been sacked?'

I shook my head. She looked small and tired, and her skin was very yellow in the cold grey light.

'You will be,' she said. 'I'm going to collect my papers now. They don't need girls to make their bombs and bullets now, do they? Not now they've won their stupid war.'

'Oh, Jess. What will you . . . ?'

She shrugged. 'I'm going to live with my brother Tom.' Tom was the one who was in prison for refusing to fight. Jess had told me all about it once she knew that I'd found out. 'When he gets out, you know. I'll look for some cheap lodgings down by the docks and get a job somewhere. I'll be all right.'

'And the Rockets?'

Jess shook her head. 'It's the end, Lil. We're all being laid off and they're not going to let us play on the men's grounds, are they? Not now they've got their proper footballers back from the front. Nobody's going to want to watch the women's game any more.'

'You don't know that.'

'Trust me, Lil,' she said. 'I do.'

And then she turned and went into the office.

I called after her: 'Jess? Jess!' But she didn't look back.

'Scared?' said Dad.

It was the morning of my first game with Spurs and we were in the kitchen. Dad was drinking tea and I was staring hopelessly at a boiled egg. My mouth was too dry to speak, so I just mumbled something in response. To my surprise, Dad grinned.

'Good girl,' he said. 'Only stupid people are never scared. And my girl is not stupid. Just go with it, Lil. Let the fear trickle through you. Once you're out there, you'll be fine.'

I tried to smile but couldn't.

'You'll be wanting to get there good and early, I'm thinking,' he went on. 'To avoid the changing room?'

I nodded, still unable to speak.

'So?' said Dad.

'So,' I said. Then I got up and patted his shoulder. He put his hand over mine for a moment.

'We'll be there, love,' he said. 'Bill's coming round to pick me up later. So don't worry. Whatever happens, we'll be there.'

The day had started off freezing cold and foggy, and by the time I got to White Hart Lane the fog was so thick that you could barely see from one end of the ground to the other. I was relieved to find that none of the other players had arrived, so I got changed quickly and headed out on to the pitch with a ball. I'd told Mr Grimshaw that I liked to get out early on my own to warm up, and he seemed to accept that. Goalkeepers had a reputation for being oddballs, loners, a bit different. They just didn't know quite how different Charlie Dodd was, and I certainly wasn't going to let them find out.

Mr Grimshaw was standing on the touchline, in his hat and overcoat, staring gloomily into the fog that rolled over the pitch like smoke. 'Ah, Dodd,' he said. 'It's not looking good, I'm afraid. Can't see the referee letting us play in this.'

'No, sir,' I said and banged the ground with the heel of my boot. It was rock hard. The pitch had got churned up during training, and the mud had frozen into peaks and furrows. It looked more like a ploughed field than a football pitch. I bounced the ball on it and it flew off at a funny angle.

'Just as well in a way,' Mr Grimshaw went on. 'You'd have had to play the whole game.'

My heart turned over in my chest, whether from excitement or fear I couldn't tell.

'Sir?' I said.

The manager took a neatly folded handkerchief out of his overcoat pocket and blew his nose with a big honking sound. 'Gorman's had an accident,' he said, carefully folding the handkerchief up again. Gorman was the first goalkeeper. 'Came off his bicycle on his way to work, apparently,' he went on. 'Sprained his ankle. He'll be out of action for a while, possibly till the start of the new season.'

So now I was Tottenham Hotspurs' only keeper. I stood there, unable to speak, my breath adding to the fog as Mr Grimshaw tucked his handkerchief back in his pocket and rubbed his moustache with his forefinger.

'Makes no odds for today's game, mind,' he said. 'We can't play in these conditions. Referee's bound to call it off.'

The referee didn't call it off. By the time he arrived the fog had cleared a bit, and a pale wintry sun was beginning to come through. He and Mr Grimshaw walked around the pitch together, hacking at the mud with the heels of their boots and frowning at the sky. My teammates had started to arrive too, and were hanging about on the sidelines shaking their heads. I just carried on warming up, too shy to speak to any of them. Part of me was desperate to play and part of me was praying the game would be cancelled. But it wasn't up to me, and by the time the opposition had arrived, the referee had made his decision. The game was going ahead.

Billy stuck his head into the changing room a few minutes before kick-off to pick up my outdoor clothes so I could go straight home afterwards. 'The ground's nearly full,' he said. 'Me and your dad are in the west stand. And Wilfred, of course.'

'Thanks, Bill.'

Some of the other players remembered him from the trial, and looked up from lacing their boots and adjusting their shin pads to say hello.

'Good luck, lads,' he said. 'Show them what you're made of, Charlie.' A wink, and he was gone.

I was on my own.

It was strange feeling. In one way, everything was familiar. The changing room that smelt just like the one at the old Manor Ground, of mud and sweat, trampled grass and leather. The tension that makes players crack stupid jokes and tease each other. The sense of being together, but also apart. A feeling of loyalty to your teammates that was almost like love, but at the same time the hope that you'll look good, better than them, that people will think you're the best player on the pitch. But it was also different, so different from the last time I played as part of a team, with the Rockets at the old Manor Ground. I was a professional now, playing in a professional team. I was being paid to play football.

And I was a girl.

It was time to go out. We lined up, me in my place at the back. The crowd roared, ghostly in the fog. The referee tossed a coin and we won. Our captain pointed the way he wanted us to play and we took up our positions. The other players trotted to their places, but I walked, shoulders back, head held high. The Duchess of Pilkington on her way to her goal.

I was ready.

The fog was getting thicker. It swirled around the players' legs, sucking the colour out of everything. Even the grass looked grey, and the roars of the crowd sounded as if they were coming from the other side of the world. All I could see was the outline of the stands on each side of the pitch, like great ships in the fog. I was glad to know Dad and Billy were there, but quite glad I couldn't see them. I made a big show of checking the nets at the back of my goal and then nodded to the referee. He gave a thumbs-up to me and then to the keeper at the other end. I took up position in front of my goal and waited for the whistle.

It was nearly time.

Time's a funny thing. Sometimes it feels like four years can go by in a flash, and sometimes a minute can last a hundred years. At last the whistle came, sharp as a pin through the fog. There was another ghostly roar from the crowd and the game began.

It was like playing in a dream. We had the best of it at first, play was mostly in their half. I could see my two full-backs drifting up the pitch into the fog, following the play, while I waited on my line, shifting from foot to foot in the icy mud, watching, waiting. *Expect the unexpected, Lily-oh*, Dad always used to say, *expect the unexpected*.

So I did. And, as usually happens, the unexpected came.

A lone player appeared out of the fog on my left, taking my full-backs by surprise. He came tearing down the wing towards me, the ball stuck to his feet like glue. I never knew a player could move so fast.

'Fred!' I yelled. 'FRED!'

Fred was my left-back, an old school player from up north, an amateur, big, heavy, dependable, but not fast, and he was getting a bit too old for the game.

'Away!' I shouted. 'Away!'

I came out of my goal, preparing to take the player on myself if necessary, but Fred moved in for the tackle. He was nothing if not brave. There was a horrible crash as the Clapton player clattered into him and they both went down on to the freezing mud.

The whistle cut though the fog. Our free kick. Fred took it, booting the ball long and hard down the pitch. I watched it disappear, glad of a few seconds' respite. Then it was back, appearing as if from nowhere, heading straight for my goal. It was an easy save. I scooped the ball up easily and threw it to Fred.

The crowd roared. I realized I was happy, happier than I'd felt for a long time. I forgot everything: my dad's blindness, Amy kissing Jack, Jess losing her job, the end of the Rockets. Nothing else mattered but the game. It was like being invisible.

And then another whistle came out of the fog. I strained to see what was happening, but could only see ghostly grey figures moving vaguely in and out of view.

'Fred?'

The big full-back looked over his shoulder.

'What's going on?'

'We're making a change,' he said. 'Someone's hurt.'

He jerked his head towards the touchline, where a ghostly player was warming up, making short runs up and down, the fog swirling around him.

'A change?' I said. 'I thought we didn't have any subs.'

'He's just arrived,' said Fred. 'Got held up by the weather. They say he's good.'

Another whistle, and our injured player limped off. The newcomer shook his hand, then ran on to take his place as centre-forward. But not before I saw his face.

It was Jack Darling.

After the game he shook my hand.

The final whistle blew, the crowd roared, the players congratulated each other, and Jack Darling turned and walked straight towards my goal. The fog had cleared, the sky was big and blue above us, and a bitter wind was whipping round our legs. His eyes were on a level with mine, the eyes that I'd stared into a thousand times while they looked unseeingly into mine from the photograph I kept in the old biscuit tin under my bed. It still smelt faintly of biscuits, that tin, and I seemed to smell them now on that bitter day in north London as I held Jack Darling's hand.

His eyes were blue. I'd always thought they were brown.

A thought suddenly dropped into my head. *He looks like me*, it said. *He looks. Like me.* And he did, a bit. Not me then, when I was Lily the munitionette, but me now, Charlie Dodd the goalie.

We stood there in silence, a still point in the world, with the wind and the crowd roaring around us. For a moment I was scared he'd be able to read my mind, see me for what I was – not the goalkeeper who had kept his team in the game, but the girl who'd been writing to him and then stopped because she was jealous of her best friend.

That was the first time I realized what it was, the thing I'd felt when I saw Amy kiss him at the zoo, that I'd been feeling ever since. The first time I gave it a name.

Jealousy. It was called jealousy.

'I'm Jack,' he said. 'Jack Darling.' Behind his confident smile, his eyes had an anxious look, and there was a scar down the side of his face that wasn't there in the photograph. I realized I was still holding his hand, so I let go of it quickly.

'I know,' I said. The words came out before I could stop them, and I felt my cheeks burn at my own stupidity. Luckily, he was vain enough to think that I just knew his reputation as a footballer, so he smiled.

'Good game,' he said. We'd won, one-nil. I'd made a couple of decent saves and Jack had scored our goal. 'My first since I got back,' he added. 'I've been...'

'I know,' I said again, and felt even more stupid.

'Well played, Dodd.' Someone slapped me on the back. I turned to see Fred Butterworth, the big left-back. 'Not bad for a first game,' he added and strode off towards the clubhouse.

Jack turned his head and looked at me sideways.

'Dodd?' he said. His eyes were on my face. *He couldn't know*, I thought. *How could he?* It was a common enough name, and he'd never seen me before.

'Yes,' I squeaked, and laughed nervously before remembering to lower my voice. 'Charlie Dodd, at your service!' That was stupid, but I carried on blindly. 'I just got signed, from Woolwich.'

Jack shook his head and ran his hand over his curls, scattering drops of water. There was mud on his face. 'Funny,' he said. 'I had a friend...' Then he stopped and let his eyes rest on a couple of little boys who'd got hold of a ball from somewhere and were taking shots into my goal.

'Yes?' I said, eagerness making my voice squeak again.

He sighed. 'Nothing,' he said. We stood there for a moment in silence and then he added, 'You going to stand here all night?' and I remembered where I was. The other players had all gone back to the clubhouse and the crowds were filing out of the ground. Bill was waving to me from the front of the north stand, and Dad was next to him, with Wilf under his coat.

'Hey, Charlie!' Bill shouted. 'Charlie Dodd!'

'It's my dad,' I said to Jack. 'I'd better go and say hello. First game and everything.'

Jack nodded, a muscle twitching at the side of his face. I wondered what he'd seen to cause that twitch. 'Dads are important,' he said. Then he slapped my arm, a light friendly slap that wasn't really a slap at all. 'And you had a good game, Charlie Dodd,' he said. 'Well done, mate.'

I stood there watching him move off through the mist. The place where he'd touched my arm felt warm, I could almost feel the imprint of his hand.

'Charlie! Charlie Dodd!'

Billy was still shouting to me, so I went over to handshakes and laughter and Bill's eyes dancing and my dad's face. He reached across and touched my cheek.

'All right?' he said.

I realized I'd been holding my breath. 'Yes, Dad,' I said. 'I'm fine.'

Bill was too full of the game to notice how quiet I was on the train home.

'It was you, Charlie,' he said. He seemed to have got quite used to my new name. 'You won that game.'

I shook my head. 'I don't know about that.'

'Nah, without that save in the second half it would've ended in a draw.' He turned to Dad. 'She just flipped it away, Mr Dodd, easy as pie—'

'Bill . . .' I shot him a warning look. He might have got used to calling me Charlie, but he still couldn't think of me as 'he'.

'Oops, sorry,' he said. '*He* just flipped it away, I mean.' He laughed, but I looked around the carriage nervously. There was a soldier in uniform and a girl whispering together across the aisle, and two women with shopping baskets complaining about the price of butter. Nobody was interested in me.

Dad reached out and patted my mud-caked knee. 'I'm proud of you,' he said. And then he added, 'son,' and Bill laughed.

'Thanks, Dad,' I said. I took his big rough hand and held it in mine, just like I'd held Jack Darling's after the game.

Bill rattled on, excited at everything. 'That centre-forward they brought on, he's a good player,' he said. 'That's the one I was telling you about, Mr Dodd, just back from the front. Footballers' Battalion.' Dad nodded and Bill went on, looking at me. 'Bloke next to me said he'd been with Spurs before the war, since he was a kid . . .'

'Lucky to have come back,' said Dad. 'So many haven't. What did you say his name was, Bill?'

'Darling,' I said, before Bill could open his mouth. 'His name's Jack Darling.'

When we got back to Spray Street, Billy went out for fish and chips and I filled up the tin bath in front of the fire and took off my muddy kit. I put the wooden clothes airer around the bath and hung it with blankets so I had some privacy. When I'd had my bath and was wrapped up in an old dressing gown of Dad's and the three of us had eaten our fish suppers, I left Bill and Dad in the kitchen talking about the game and went up to my room.

The biscuit tin where I kept Jack's letters was still there, under the bed where I'd left it. I hadn't looked in it properly since the day I followed Amy May to the zoo and my hands were trembling as I opened the lid. There he was, looking at me out of the photograph, laughing into my eyes, looking so young and so happy. He didn't look like that now. I touched his face with one finger, wondering if he'd ever look that happy again. I turned the old letters over, reading the odd phrase here and there. His mate Harry, the goalkeeper from Brighton who used to catch the bombs as they came over the side of the trench and lob them back to the enemy before they went off; the perfect cottage garden they'd come across in a ruined village where he'd picked a pansy and sent it to me; the games, the tournaments, the matches that they always won. And then there were the letters I'd never opened, the ones he'd sent after the day at the zoo, still unread, still in their envelopes. I picked one up and looked at the postmark. April 1918. The first one he'd written after he'd met Amy. I turned it over and looked at the back. Should I open it?

'Lily!' Dad was calling me from downstairs. He was pretty good at getting round the house on his own now, so he didn't need my help, but I went out on to the landing anyway.

'I'm here, Dad.'

He was at the bottom of the stairs, his face turned up towards me.

'Bill's gone home,' he said. 'He said to say goodbye.'

'All right. Thanks.' I turned back to my room.

'I'm proud of you, Lil,' Dad said before I got there. 'Very proud.' He swallowed as if something was sticking in his throat. 'But . . . is everything all right?'

'Yes. Why? What do you mean?' I went down to him.

'I don't know, love. You seem . . .'

I took his arm and together we went back to the kitchen, where Wilfred was standing on a chair with his paws on the table, snuffling though the chip papers for scraps. I shooed him off and sat Dad down, then pulled up the chair next to him and took his hand.

'Really, Dad,' I said, looking into his unseeing eyes. 'Everything's fine. I've got a job doing what I love and I seem to be getting away with it. How many girls can say that? Or boys, come to that.'

He laughed. 'Sounds like you're more than getting away with it, love,' he said. 'Sounds like you're outplaying these blokes at their own game.' And then he stopped laughing and patted the back of my hand. 'It's just . . . you don't seem very happy about it, Lil. And I don't know why.'

CHAPTER

TWENTY-TWO

The weeks went by. Christmas came and went, the weather grew colder, and Jack and I became friends. Friends! We laughed together, trained together, teased each other and slapped each other on the back from time to time.

That was all.

The other lads had got used to me too. They accepted that I was always out on the pitch warming up before they arrived, and I always left straight after training or a game, with Billy and my dad. That was just the way I was. A bit odd. A loner. Goalkeepers were like that, part of the team, but always on their own.

'Old Charlie, he's a bit of a strange one.'

'Off home already, Charlie?'

'As per usual.'

I was a good goalkeeper, that helped. It also helped that they knew about Dad, how he'd lost his sight in the air raid and that I had to get home to look after him. They didn't ask questions, so I didn't have to lie, and that was the way I liked it. We couldn't all be good liars like Amy May.

I was friends with all of them. I liked them and I think they liked me. But there was something different between me and Jack. We never talked, not really. (I wouldn't have known how to talk as a boy, actually, not have a proper conversation. I could play football like one, but I had no idea how they talked together when no one else was around.) We never spent time together off the pitch, but there was something between us. I'd noticed it the first moment we met, when Jack had heard my name was Dodd. Perhaps it was my imagination, but I felt he still looked at me in a different way, and when he shook my hand after a game, or patted me on the back when I'd made a particularly good save, his hand seemed to linger a bit longer than it needed to.

But as I say, perhaps it was my imagination.

The other players saw Jack as a bit of a strange one too, so it seemed natural that we became friends. There were a couple of others who'd been out at the front, but they hadn't been in the trenches as long as Jack. We all understood why he could lose his temper over nothing, and pretended not to notice when his hands shook and his eyes sometimes seemed to look at things that weren't there.

I asked Dad once if he could still see, now his eyes didn't work any more. It sounds like a funny question, but he knew what I meant straight away.

"Course I can,' he said. 'I can see your face as clear as day. The blue sky—'

'It's grey, Dad. This is London.'

'The grey sky.' He grinned. 'Your mum's smile.' He paused for a moment and I knew he was picturing it. I could see it too, but the smile I saw was the one in the photograph. Dad was seeing the real thing.

He gave his head a little shake and carried on. 'The look in this little dog's eyes when he's begging for his grub.' Wilfred was sitting on his lap, even though he was really too big for that now. Dad scratched his ears. 'I might be blind, Lil,' he said. 'But I'm not *blind*.'

I laughed at that, and then he laughed, and I said, 'So what does my face look like now, Dad? Right now this minute.'

And I pulled a funny face at him, crossing my eyes and sticking out my tongue.

'Hm.' Dad pretended to think. 'I reckon . . . you've got your eyes crossed . . . and your tongue sticking out the corner of your mouth.' He turned to me and grinned. 'Am I right?'

'How do you *know* that?'

Dad tapped the side of his nose. 'I know *you*, Lily Dodd,' he said. 'And that's the face you always used to pull behind my back when you were a little girl and I told you we had to stop playing football and go home for tea. You thought I couldn't see you, didn't you?'

I nodded, then said, 'Yes.'

'And you think I can't see you now. But I can.'

And that was how it was with Jack. He saw things that were invisible to everyone else. Whenever there was a lull in a game or a break in training, I'd see his eyes looking at something nobody else could see, and I don't think it was a girl pulling a funny face. I wondered what he'd seen out there in France, and wished I knew how to ask him, or whether it would even help if I did. *Amy would know what to say*, I thought. But then Amy always did.

We had another friendly a couple of weeks later, this time against a team from up north, one of the Sheffield clubs. It was a scrappy game, nasty and bad-tempered. Mr Grimshaw was a Yorkshireman himself and he told us that northern teams like to see us Londoners as a bit soft, and are always keen to prove it. This team was no exception. I lost count of the times I got clattered by their forwards, and watched helplessly as my defenders were pulled about and tripped and kicked behind the referee's back. I could see Jack getting angry, but there was nothing any of us could do but battle on. Their players were big and tough and determined, and for the first part of the game most of the play was in our half. I made a few decent saves and we got through to half-time with a nil-nil score.

Then the referee blew his whistle for the start of the second half. We started well. Our forwards had the wind behind them and the Sheffield players got more and more desperate. I watched Jack as he was kicked and shoved, and held back by his jersey, time after time turning to the referee, struggling to control his temper. It was nearly full-time and we were still holding them to nil-nil when Jack made a quick run back to pick up a ball in our half and one of their players moved to block him. There was a nasty tackle and they both went down. The whistle went.

Free kick. To them. Jack went white with fury. I was afraid for him.

Their centre-forward stepped up to take the kick. He was a big man, fast and strong and powerful. He looked at me. I looked at him. He knew that he could reach my goal with his kick, and I knew it too. The crowd roared and I heard Dad's voice:

Let it flow through you, Lily. The fear, the anger, the noise of the crowd. Let it flow through you like water.

I tried, but this time I couldn't do it. I kept thinking of Jack. His head was down and I knew he thought it was his fault, that he'd given away this free kick because he was angry, and I wanted to tell him that it didn't matter.

The whistle blew.

I thought of Dad in the stand, with Wilf in his arms and Bill beside him, his mouth close to his ear, describing what was happening above the roar of the crowd, the rackety-racket of the football rattles. I heard Dad's voice again. *Watch the player, Lily. Watch the player, not the ball.*

I watched the player.

He took his run-up, dropped his right shoulder and drew his leg back to make the shot. He was clever. I could usually guess the angle the ball was coming, but not this time. I made myself as big as I could, picturing myself filling the entire goal with my body.

I heard the hollow bang of his boot as it struck the ball and the ball flew. I jumped for it, arms spread wide, hanging in the air for what felt like minutes, and then felt a horrible thud as it hit my chest. I flew backwards, unable to reach the ball with my hands, and crashed to the ground. The ball bounced off. I'd saved it, hadn't I? I curled up on the ground, feeling the pain now, and saw the big centre-forward's boots by my face, tapping the ball past me into my goal.

The whistle blew. The game was over. We'd lost, one-nil. And Jack had disappeared.

I looked around. The spectators were filing out of the stands, players were celebrating, slapping each other on the back, or shaking their heads and commiserating with each other. I caught a glimpse of Bill and Dad standing very still on the touchline as the centre-forward who'd scored came up and shook my hand.

'Good game, pal,' he said. I nodded absently, my eyes scanning the pitch. Where was he? Where was Jack?

'Nobody could've stopped that shot, Charlie.' Fred had come over to commiserate. 'Don't let it bother you.'

'I won't, Fred,' I said. 'Thanks. I've just got to . . .'

And I left him standing there by my goal as I legged it across to the edge of the pitch where I'd just seen Jack Darling disappear through a small door in the fence at the side of the north stand.

I emerged through the door to find myself in an ordinary quiet street of grey London houses dozing in the chilly afternoon light. An old man in a cap, sitting on a low wall, smoking. A scruffy black-and-white dog, sniffing at a lamp post. A woman shaking a yellow duster out of a first-floor window. Three little girls with cold bare legs, skipping, two holding the red wooden handles at either end of the rope while the other jumped in the middle. The slap of the rope on the road and the sound of their voices echoed in the damp air:

'*Salt, mustard, vinegar, PEPPER.*'

I looked to the right. There was no sign of Jack Darling.

'*Salt, mustard, vinegar, PEPPER.*'

I looked to the left. It was as if he'd disappeared into thin air. I stood there for a minute, catching my breath and wondering what to do, when I saw the dog disappear into a gap between two of the houses. There must be an alleyway there that I couldn't see from where I was standing. I ran towards it, my boots ringing on the pavement, dodging round the girls, who stopped their skipping to stare at me, and the old man, who spat on the pavement as I passed. The alleyway stretched a long way between the houses and their back yards, between high brick walls, blackened with soot and smoke. And there, striding away from me at the far end, was Jack.

I ran after him, the sound of my boots echoing off the high walls on either side of the alleyway. A dirty-looking white cat flicked her tail as I passed, and a snail shell crunched under my foot.

'Jack!' I shouted. 'Jack Darling!' Either he didn't hear me or he pretended not to, because he didn't stop, so I called again. 'It's Charlie, mate! Wait for me!'

This time he stopped. He stood there for a moment, his back stiff and straight, then turned and looked at me over his shoulder.

'Where are you going?' I yelled.

But he didn't reply. Just shook his head and carried on walking.

'Jack!'

I caught up with him on a scrubby bit of waste ground at the end of the alleyway. People had made some of it into allotments to grow vegetables during the war, I supposed, but there wasn't much growing there now. Just piles of rubbish and dead plants and sticks that had been used to support peas or beans. There were even a few ramshackle sheds that had been nailed together from old doors and random bits of wood from bombed-out buildings, still with traces of their old paint, yellow, green and black. An old man was leaning on a spade, looking thoughtfully at some dead-looking cabbages, and the dog that had brought me here was sniffing around an old iron bedstead that looked like someone had tried to set it on fire. The whole place smelt of damp and rotten cabbages.

Jack was sitting on a home-made bench, staring at nothing. I sat down next to him. The wood felt splintery and rough against the back of my knees. Jack didn't look at me, but shifted himself slightly to make space. I didn't know what to say, so I held out my hand to the dog who'd trotted over to see if we had any food to give him.

'Good dog,' I said, and then felt stupid for saying something so obvious. The dog wagged his tail. He looked at me, then looked at Jack and then looked back at me again. *So you haven't got any food for me*, he said to me with his eyes, *but perhaps this person has. What d'you think?*

I shook my head. The dog sat down and rested

his chin thoughtfully on Jack's knee. Jack reached out a hand and let it rest on the dog's head, his eyes still fixed on something in the distance that I couldn't see. The shriek of a faraway train echoed in the silence, followed by the distant rhythm of its wheels.

'I used to come up here when I was a kid,' Jack said, still looking straight ahead. 'None of this was here then.' With his free hand he indicated the tumble of sheds and rubbish. 'It was just a bit of rough ground where we could play football.'

'I didn't know you grew up round here,' I said, glad he'd broken the silence.

He nodded, his hand in the dog's rough fur. 'Used to go and see Spurs with my dad,' he said. 'Every Sunday when they were at home, regular as clockwork.'

'Me too,' I said. 'Only it was Woolwich Arsenal for us.' I felt stupid again.

The daylight was starting to thicken into dusk and the air felt like a damp blanket, thick and pale and cold. I shivered. My jersey was still clammy with sweat from the game, and now it was beaded all over with drops of moisture from the damp air.

Jack sighed, feeling the dog's soft ears between

his fingers, and closed his eyes as if he was trying to shut something out. When he opened them it was as if a light had been turned on. He turned to look at me for the first time.

'You got a girl, Charlie?' he said.

I drew back, surprised at the bluntness of his question.

'No,' I said, stupidly. Then, with an embarrassed laugh, 'Not yet, anyway.'

His eyes shifted back to look into the distance. The old man had given up on his cabbages, and went into his shed to put his spade away.

'I had one once,' said Jack. 'At least, I thought I did.'

I couldn't speak. A cold feeling of dread spread from my stomach up to my shoulders. He was going to tell me about Amy, I knew he was. And that was something I really didn't want to hear.

Jack turned to face me on the bench, moving the dog's head off his knee.

'Her name was Dodd too,' he said. 'Like yours.' He shook his head. 'And she used to write to me, you know, when I was out at the front. Her letters were the only things that kept me going. Well, them and the football. And . . .'

He stopped. I swallowed, still unable to speak.

'But sometimes there was no football,' Jack went on. 'There was just . . .' He gave a shudder and shook his head as if he was trying to shoo a fly away, but the memory was still in his eyes and his hands were trembling. 'I loved getting her letters,' he said after a moment. 'They were just so . . . *real*.' He turned to look at me again, his blue eyes shining as if he'd just discovered something wonderful. 'D'you know what I mean?'

I nodded dumbly, feeling my eyes prick with stupid tears.

'She wouldn't send me a photograph,' he said. 'Even though I begged and begged. Perhaps she couldn't afford to get one done, I don't know. So I never knew what she looked like. And then she stopped writing. Just stopped.'

There was a silence while the dog sniffed around our feet, and then Jack turned to me suddenly, as if he thought I might know the answer to the question he was about to ask. Which of course I did. 'Why did she have to stop writing, Charlie? Those letters meant the world to me. I thought of going round her house when I got back. But then I got scared. Scared that something had happened to her. She worked at the Arsenal and, you know . . . if something did happen to her there, well, I didn't want to know.'

The old man had locked up his shed and was trudging up the path towards us, whistling tunelessly between his teeth. The dog looked up.

'So you . . . never saw her?' I managed to say.

Jack's eyes were on the burnt-out bedstead. 'Once,' he said. I held my breath. 'One day when I was on leave. We met in London. We went to the zoo.' The old man walked past us and whistled for the dog, who got up with a tired sigh and trotted after him. Jack waited until they were out of sight, then turned to look at me. 'But, Charlie,' he said, 'it wasn't her!'

What? I thought. And then, 'What?' I said, my voice shaking so much I could hardly get the word out.

'Oh, she was nice,' said Jack. 'She was pretty. She was sweet. I liked her, you know? I really liked her. But I could tell. I just knew. She wasn't the girl who'd been writing to me.'

'How could you know?' I said. And then, that horrible thought. 'She didn't tell you, did she?'

Jack shook his head, then reached into the top of his sock and pulled out a tiny tin box, the sort that had those little liquorice sweets in when you were a kid. I had one that I used for my baby teeth when they fell out. Jack's was all bashed up and bent, with most of the paint scratched off. He prised open the lid and held it out in the palm of his hand.

'Look,' he said.

I looked. There was nothing inside. The box was completely empty. I began to be afraid that he'd really lost his mind.

'I found it in one of her letters,' he said. 'I don't suppose she even knew it was there.'

'Found what? Jack, there's nothing there, mate. It—' I stopped because Jack had carefully picked something out of the bottom of the box. It was a single coiled hair, very long, very wiry. Very red.

It was my hair.

'The girl I met was blonde,' Jack said. 'It wasn't her. So tell me, Charlie. Where's the girl this hair belongs to? And who is the girl I met?'

CHAPTER TWENTY-THREE

What could I say? I argued with him, of course I did. That hair he found in the bottom of the envelope, I said, that single long, wiry, red hair, it might not have belonged to the girl who wrote the letters. It could've come from anywhere. Perhaps it belonged to the girl's mum, her sister, her friend?

Oh, I was getting good at lying. Amy May would've been proud of me.

Jack shrugged. 'I don't know, Charlie. I just didn't feel like the girl I met was the girl who wrote those letters.'

We sat there in silence for a minute. The lamps were coming on in the streets beyond the waste ground, one after another, their blue light shining mistily through the dusk, turning the streets into strings of beads.

'She stopped writing after the day we met,' Jack said, his eyes on the lights in the distance. 'She never wrote again.'

I tried to make a joke of it. 'Perhaps she didn't like what she saw!'

'Perhaps.' He sighed. 'It changed everything, you know.'

'How d'you mean?'

'When she stopped writing. I didn't care any more. Couldn't care less about what happened to me, about anything really.' Somewhere a dog started to bark. 'It makes you go a bit funny if you're out there too long,' Jack went on. 'I had a friend—' He stopped suddenly as if someone had whispered in his ear, then nodded to himself, his eyes still on the distant lights. 'Harry,' he said. He didn't know I already knew his friend's name, how could he? 'He was a goalkeeper, like you.' He gave me a quick look from the corner of his eye. 'Brighton and Hove Albion.' I waited for him to go on. 'He walked into the enemy fire, Charlie. Climbed out of the trench one morning and just walked. Straight towards their guns.' Jack's face was twitching. 'I tried to stop him,' he said. 'I shouted, grabbed his legs, but it was no good. He'd had enough.' Jack turned his face to mine for a moment but his eyes weren't looking at me. 'Felt like it myself sometimes, after she stopped writing.' He laughed and then stopped laughing. 'Silly, eh?' he said.

I shook my head, unable to speak. Jack's best mate, Harry, the funny goalkeeper who'd caught the bombs the Germans sent over and lobbed them back to them, had been killed, and in such an awful way. A tear fell on my shorts. I watched the little blob of wetness spread on the dark blue fabric.

Jack rubbed his hand over his face and sighed. 'But that girl,' he said. 'That girl who wrote those letters.' He turned towards me, moonlight all over his face.

'I miss her, Charlie. She was my pal.'

Dad and Billy were waiting for me when I walked through the door, still in my muddy football kit.

'Bill brought your clothes back, Lil,' said Dad

when I'd sat down. He reached out and found my hand. 'Bad luck with the game, love,' he added. 'You can't win 'em all.'

'What happened to you?' Bill sounded almost angry. 'Where did you go? We were worried.'

'It was Jack Darling,' I said. 'You know, our centre-forward, the one that just got back from France? He went a bit funny. Walked off, so I went to find him.'

Bill made an impatient little huffing noise, but Dad nodded. 'Poor lad. He's seen things nobody should ever see. Not at his age. Not at any age.' He squeezed my hand. 'You're a good friend to him, Lily, I can see that. A very good friend.'

The next game was the big one. It was still a friendly, of course, but an important one, against Spurs' great rivals, the Arsenal. I'd be playing against my own home team.

Bill had come round to have breakfast with us before I left on the morning of the match. 'What d'you reckon, Mr Dodd?' he said. 'Who are you putting your money on today?'

Dad smiled and turned to where I was sitting at

the table, washing down my third boiled egg with a gallon of scalding tea. 'I never thought I'd say this, Bill,' he said. 'But I don't think the Arsenal have got a hope in hell of pulling this one off. Not with this girl in goal.'

'See you later, Dad.' I kissed his head. 'Bill.' I grabbed my old jacket and my boots, gave them a little wave and swung out, slamming the front door behind me.

I'd got to the ground early as usual, and was warming up on the pitch with our coach when he suddenly stopped, the ball in his hands, and looked around. 'Heads up, Dodd,' he said. 'The opposition's arrived.'

A few of the Arsenal players had emerged from their changing room, kicking a ball to each other and laughing. I hadn't seen them play for years, not since Dad and I used to go and watch them on the old Manor Ground in Plumstead when they were Woolwich Arsenal and I was a little girl, so there was no one there I recognized. They kept to the far end of the pitch, passing the ball between them and taking shots for their keeper to save.

Their keeper.

I went icy cold.

'Dodd?' The coach had his foot on the ball, waiting to take a shot. 'You all right?'

The keeper at the other end of the pitch was bouncing on his feet in his goal, joking with his teammates, catching the ball and throwing it back to them with one-handed ease. I stood there, staring, rooted to the spot.

'Dodd!' The coach's voice seemed to be coming from a long way away. 'What's up, mate?' he said. 'You look like you've seen a ghost.'

I opened my mouth to speak, but nothing came out. I didn't know what to say, because it was true. I had seen a ghost. A ghost from my past. The Arsenal keeper was my old enemy from the factory.

It was Joe Crawford.

Crawford wouldn't know it was me, I told myself. How could he? I hadn't recognized him at first, so how would he recognize me, dressed as a boy, with my hair cut short? He was over a hundred yards away in his goal, so as long as we each kept to our own areas, he'd never get close enough to see my face. It would be fine. It had to be.

And so the game began. It seemed like all of north London had come out to watch. I didn't think many supporters of the old Woolwich Arsenal would make the trip across the river, but I knew Dad was behind my goal, sitting on a bench at the front of the stand with Wilfred on his lap and Billy Cracken beside him, and that made me feel a bit better.

I stood on my line, protecting my goal, watching, waiting, trying to forget about Crawford, to concentrate on the game. We can win this, I told myself, we have to. And for the first few minutes we had the better of them. Jack had seemed happier, or at least less strange, since we'd talked the previous week, and he was playing like a madman. I'd always known he was fast, but now, with the ball at his feet and the wind behind him, he went ghosting through the Arsenal defence time after time until only Crawford was between him and the goal. But Crawford was a good keeper and Jack was out on his own up there, none of our other forwards could keep up with him. Time after time, Jack struck the ball, and Crawford saved it.

But a goal was coming. We knew it and so did they.

I watched, I waited, and it happened. Crawford had scooped up the ball and booted it down the pitch, like he always did. But this time Jack had run back and he was waiting. He stopped the ball with his chest, directing it to his feet, and ran with it again. It seemed like nobody could stop him that day, nobody could get near him, let alone take the ball off him. Two of our forwards were still up there, waiting, dodging around the Arsenal defenders, waiting for Jack. He was through, he ran past them, nudged the ball to them, they passed it back to him and BOOM! Crawford leapt for it, but it flew over his head, grazed the tips of his fingers and hit the back of the net.

One-nil. To us.

We didn't celebrate. We'd earned it fair and square. We were the better team, we knew that. Arsenal were beginning to smell beaten.

But it was close. By half-time, Arsenal had won a corner.

'Away!' I shouted at my defenders. They were so keen to protect our lead that they were gathered around the goal, blocking my view of play. 'Away!

Away!' But it was too late. The referee blew his whistle and the ball came, a high swinging cross. I needed to come out of my goal to collect it, but I was blocked by my own defenders. The ball was coming, coming, and all I could do was push my way through, leap and punch it away, just like I did that summer's day long ago when I'd just started working at the Arsenal and I saved the lady visitor's feathery hat.

The ball was away, but not far enough. My defenders weren't quick enough to reach it, but the Arsenal centre-forward was. He headed it into my goal. I didn't have a chance.

One all. The whistle blew.

'We can do this, lads,' Mr Grimshaw told us in the changing room at half-time. 'Their goal was lucky. Ours was deserved. We're better than them. Just keep your heads up and we'll be home and dry. All right, out you go and show them what you're made of.'

The other players gave a little cheer and headed out to the pitch for the second half, but I hung back. I looked at my face in the stained and spotted mirror that hung on the wall. It was all very well for Mr Grimshaw to tell us to show them what we were made of, but what was I made of? I wasn't sugar and spice or slugs and snails. Who was I? Was I Charlie Dodd, goalkeeper, Jack Darling's best mate? Or Lily, the girl who'd been writing to him? And then, as I looked at my familiar face in the mirror, the face I'd stared at a thousand times and wished it was different, the truth came to me in a flash. I wasn't Charlie or Lily. I was neither of them and both of them at the same time.

I was me.

We held them to one-all, but we couldn't score. Jack seemed tired. It was if he'd used up all his energy in the first half, and although our supporters were roaring encouragement, the wind was against us and we couldn't get through. I could just make out Bill and Dad in the crowd behind the opposite goal. Bill was waving and seemed to be trying to tell me something, but I couldn't work out what. I had no time, I had to concentrate all my energy on willing on my team. I waited. I watched. I paced my line, willing us on. *Come on, come on, come on.* The minutes ticked away, but our forwards seemed hypnotized. They kept drifting back into our half, letting our opponents run the game.

And then, two minutes before the final whistle, everything changed.

Jack intercepted a lazy pass between two of their forwards and started to run. Nobody could stop him when he was like that. But there wasn't much time. I saw the referee look at his watch. There was nobody except Crawford between Jack and the goal. Crawford was moving from side to side, sticking to his line, and then he came to a decision and came out of his goal to take on Jack. It was a brave move, and it might've worked, but as he did so, one of his defenders came galloping back and made a desperate sliding tackle. I seemed to hear the awful crunch as his boot made contact with Jack's shin and Jack went down. The crowd roared and the whistle blew.

Free kick. To us. With one minute to go.

Out of the corner of my eye I could see Mr Grimshaw on the touchline telling us to push up, push up into their half. I checked the big clock on the stand. There was no way there'd be time for them to get the ball back down the pitch to our goal and score, so I left my goal and joined the others in our opponents' half. I heard Bill's voice above the roar of the crowd: 'Go, Charlie! Go!'

I went.

Jack was hurt, but not so badly that he couldn't take the kick. It was close. Close enough for him to score if he got it right, and I knew him well enough to know he'd want to try. Crawford was organizing his defence, shouting at them to clear the way so he'd have a view of the player taking the kick, of the ball.

We pushed closer.

Jack was joking with the referee and fussing with the ball, positioning it just so, ready for the kick. I knew this was partly an act to make Crawford nervous, but Crawford was ready. Jack strolled back, casual as you like, to take his run-up. The whistle blew. Jack ran, we all moved, Jack's boot struck the ball, Crawford went for it, the defenders yelled, but I could see, I could see what was going to happen. Crawford was good, he'd read Jack's mind, tricked him by offering him a bit of space at the bottom edge of the goal, and Jack had fallen for it. I was a goalkeeper too, I could see what

Crawford had done and I could see what was going to happen.

I moved. I knew exactly where I needed to be. As the ball flew, Crawford went for it, flung himself to his right, the ball hit his chest, the crowd roared, Crawford hit the ground. And the ball bounced back and landed at my feet.

I shifted my weight and, as I drew back my leg to make the shot, Crawford looked up and met my eyes. But at that moment I didn't care. I didn't care about anything. Crawford was still on the ground when the ball hit the back of the net.

The crowd went mad. I saw a sea of waving blue scarves and football rattles, Billy punching the air, Dad's face a picture of disbelief and joy as Bill yelled in his ear to tell him what had happened and Crawford, getting up from the ground, his eyes fixed on me.

And I knew. In that moment, I knew. Crawford had recognized me.

CHAPTER TWENTY-FOUR

The game was over. The teams shook hands and headed off the pitch. And I went to find Joe Crawford.

It was the end, I knew that. The end of my football career, the end of Charlie Dodd. Joe Crawford would take great pleasure in telling the world that Tottenham Hotspur was employing a girl as a goalkeeper, so I needed to act fast. I might not be able to stop him, but I reckoned I could buy some time, for myself and for my team.

I marched straight to the Arsenal changing room and flung open the door. The players were all in there, sitting on the benches, unlacing their boots. Nobody was saying anything. The room smelt like changing rooms always smell, of mud and sweat and anxiety. I expect they smell like that all over the world. The players looked up when the door opened, puzzled at the sight of me standing there, the other team's keeper, the player whose freak goal had lost them the game.

'Wrong room, mate,' one of them started to say, then stopped when he saw my face. I scanned the room. Someone laughed nervously. Crawford was in the corner, away from the others, frozen in the act of undoing his right boot, sitting quite still, staring at me.

I said one word. 'Crawford,' I said.

He got up slowly, his eyes never leaving mine. He was a tall man, taller than me, and a lot heavier and stronger and a few months ago, perhaps even a few days ago, I would've been scared. But I wasn't scared Lily any more. I was Charlie Dodd, the goalkeeper who'd just come off their line to score the winning goal, and I wasn't scared. It was like Dad always used to say, 'You take the game to them, Lil, you get off your line and go on the attack. That's the only way to win.'

The other players stayed silent as Crawford moved slowly and deliberately over to where I was standing in the doorway and then stopped, facing me, just a little too close.

'That's me,' he said.

'Outside,' I said.

One of the other players started to make a half-hearted 'whooaahh' noise, but then stopped and looked at the floor. Crawford grinned in the silence, confident that he could get the better of me. I held the door open for him, and then followed him out.

'This way.'

I indicated a narrow passageway between the changing rooms and the main building. It led to a small area at the back, enclosed by walls on three sides, where the sun never shone and nothing grew except for slime and snails. Nobody ever went there, except me when I'd left it too late to change into my kit before the others got there and I needed some privacy.

Crawford was the first to speak. 'What'll it take,' he said. 'Is that what you want to know?'

I didn't understand, not at first. 'For what?' I said. 'What'll it take for what?'

'Me to keep my mouth shut,' he said. 'I'm

guessing that's what you want.'

So that was it. Blackmail. Crawford stepped around me, blocking the only way out.

'You've got a good thing going here, haven't you, Dodd? Regular job. Decent wage. But all it takes is for me to open my mouth and *ftttt!*' He clicked his fingers in my face. 'Can you imagine the shame? Tottenham Hotspur employing a female as a goalkeeper? They'd never dare show their faces again.' He grinned, showing a mouthful of stained and broken teeth. 'So,' he went on, 'shall we start off with half your weekly wage? Would that leave you and your daddy enough to live on?'

I felt myself go hot, then cold, with rage. Crawford took a step closer to me, backing me against the wall. He was so close I could smell his sour breath, feel it on my cheek.

'Because, let's face it, even half whatever they're paying you would be better than nothing. And nothing is what you'll get when I tell them the truth. So. What do you say? *Dodd.*'

He spat my name in my face and then smiled. For one awful moment I thought he was going to kiss me. But I didn't budge, not even to wipe his saliva off my cheek. I stared back at him, concentrating on the details of his face. Greyish skin, a sore above his right eyebrow, blackheads on his nose, lips pale beneath his thin moustache. I felt suddenly very calm. It was time to say what I'd come to say.

'But you won't do it, will you, Joe?' I said.

His mouth twisted into a sneer as he turned away from my gaze. 'Why wouldn't I?' he said. 'One word from me is all it would take. One word.'

'That's right,' I said. 'One word. One word and everyone will know. Joe Crawford was beaten by a girl.'

For a second I saw shock in his eyes, then he tried to laugh, but the laugh stuck in his throat and made him cough.

'Not for the first time, either,' I said, moving away from the wall, but keeping my eyes on him. 'Remember when you challenged Jess? Said she wasn't bad for a girl but she'd never get a shot past you, the great Joe Crawford? But, oh dear, whoops . . . *she broke your arm!*'

Crawford's face was working now, the muscles moving as if he was trying to dislodge something stuck in his teeth. He took a step back, away from me. I took a step forwards, beginning to enjoy myself.

'And now it's happened again!' I said. 'Joe Crawford, beaten by a girl! And not just any girl. A goalkeeper, like him.' I shook my head. 'What do you think your teammates would say to that, Joe? Or your manager? Or the supporters . . . just imagine what fun they'd have. Face it, Joe. You could never show your face on a football pitch again.'

Crawford turned his face away and I knew I'd won. He spat on the ground, turned and was gone, the sound of his boots ringing in the alleyway. I leant against the wall, my heart beating in my chest, and all the joy I'd felt a moment ago evaporated into the small patch of dirty white sky above me. It was over. I'd beaten Crawford, not once, but twice, I'd won that fight, but I knew it was the end. I couldn't keep up the pretence for ever. If Crawford recognized me, there'd be others. It would only be a matter of time before someone else saw the truth and embarrassed my club in front of the whole country. I couldn't let that happen.

It was over.

*

'I'm sorry, Dodd.' Mr Grimshaw was staring at me across the table. 'I thought you just said you wanted to leave the club.'

'I did, sir.'

'What, now?' he said. 'Straight away? With no notice?'

'Yes, sir,' I said. 'I'm very sorry. It's . . . difficult. I can't explain.'

He huffed air though his moustache. 'Well! It's just as well the league hasn't started up yet. If it had we'd be suing you for breach of contract.'

'I know, sir. I'm sorry.'

'Is this because Gorman's coming back next week?' Gorman was the old goalkeeper, the one who'd sprained his ankle.

'No, sir.'

'Because you might not be my first choice every week, Dodd, but after today . . .' he blew at his moustache again. 'Well, let me put it like this. There'll always be a place for you in the team.' He narrowed his eyes suddenly and looked at me over his glasses. 'Is it more money you're after?'

'No, sir!' I was horrified at the thought. 'I'm

very sorry, sir. But it's for the best. I really . . . have no choice.'

'Then . . .' Mr Grimshaw sighed and shook his head. Even his moustache looked sad. Then he straightened his shoulders and looked me in the eye. 'Very well, Dodd,' he said. 'I suppose you've got your reasons. Though I'm blowed if I can think what they are.' He reached in a drawer of the desk and counted out my wages for the last week. 'There we go,' he said as he handed them over. 'All fair and square.'

'Thank you, sir.' I stuffed the notes in the top of my sock. 'Goodbye, sir.'

Mr Grimshaw nodded and held out his hand. I took it and we shook, and then I turned away, not wanting him to see the tears in my eyes. He was a nice man.

The last of the crowd was filing out through the turnstiles when I left the building. I didn't stop to say goodbye to the team. It had been hard enough to explain to Mr Grimshaw, I could never explain to them. To Jack. So I headed for the little door at the side of the stand where I'd followed Jack the previous week. I knew Billy would've picked up my clothes from the changing room like he always did, and I just wanted to be alone. As I made my way round the edge of the pitch I saw him waving to me from the remains of the crowd in the west stand. Dad was next to him, and someone else, I couldn't see who.

'Charlie!' he yelled. 'Charlie Dodd! What a game!'

I pretended not to hear and kept on walking. I couldn't face him and Dad, not now.

'CHARLIE!' he shouted again. 'Over here! Look! LOOK!'

I was at the door now, so I opened it and went through. It was quiet in the street. The wintry sky was already showing pinkish in the west, so I turned my face to the south and I walked.

I'd been walking for half an hour before I realized I was being followed. It was a long way home from White Hart Lane, so I'd jumped on a tram for part of the way, getting off when I was close to the river. I took shortcuts, crossing parks and cutting through side roads and lanes where there weren't many people. It was in an alleyway somewhere near St Paul's that I was sure. There were footsteps behind me.

Tap. Tap. Tap.

I stopped, waited, turned. There was nobody there, just shadows and dead leaves swirling in the wind. A gritty sleet was beginning to scour the pavements. I walked on. And the footsteps started again.

Could it be Crawford? My heart beat faster at the thought. Why would he be following me? To threaten me? Hurt me? Kill me, even, anything to make me keep quiet. He would have heard by now that I'd left the club, told them I wasn't going to play for them any more, so I had nothing to lose. I could go to the newspapers, tell my story, expose him for the bully and the creep that he was.

I remembered the look in his eyes when he left me behind the clubhouse and I was scared. I kept to the busier streets after that, watching the faces go past me on the pavements, white in the cold. People leaving work, men in hats, overcoats buttoned up against the wind. There were girls too, young women, some alone and some in twos and threes, arm in arm and laughing together on their way back to their teas, their homes, their beds. Some stared at me as I strode past, this tall young boy in football kit, his knees still muddy from the game. One girl even winked and blew me a kiss from the tip of her finger, then whispered something to her friend and giggled, eyeing me as I walked past. I just stared ahead and kept on walking, still conscious of the footsteps that clicked on the pavement behind me every time I walked alone.

It was dark by the time I got to the river and the lamps were going on as I crossed the road. A motor car swerved to avoid me with a blast of its horn and a screech of its brakes, but I didn't care. I walked on, alone now, except for the river on my right and the footsteps behind me.

Tap. Tap. Tap.

I was still being followed. I could still hear the footsteps on the path, and once, when I'd turned quickly, I'd seen a dark figure flick behind a tree. I found it hard to care, hard to think about anything. So what if it was Joe Crawford? What could he do to hurt me any more than I was hurting already? The war was over, but what sort of peace was it going to be for me? I'd lost my job, my chance to play football, my best friend. My boy. I had nothing. I looked into the heaving black-and-white water of the river. Then, a tugboat chugged past, its lights blazing, breaking up the ripples and hooting a friendly greeting as it approached a bridge and the moment was gone. I remembered my dad and Billy Cracken and Wilfred, sitting together in the warm glowing kitchen in the little house in Spray Street, waiting for me, worrying about me, and I walked on.

Tap. Tap. Tap.

As I got closer to the north entrance to the foot tunnel something seemed to snap inside my head. I'd been walking for hours now. My feet were hurting, I was cold and tired, and I suddenly felt angry. I didn't care who this person was, or what they did to me. I just didn't want them following me any longer. I stopped dead still for a moment and then swung round.

There it was again. A dark figure, its head covered in a hood or something, flicking out of sight behind a lamp post. I waited. Nothing happened. There was just the slap of the water against the riverbank and the echo of a ship's siren in the distance.

'Who's there?' I said.

There was no response. I took a step towards the lamp, my heart beating hard, not with fear this time, but with anger.

'I know you're there,' I said. 'So you might as well show me who you are.'

Still nothing. I took another step.

'Or are you too scared?' I said.

Silence.

And then . . . a giggle. A familiar giggle, and Amy May stepped out from behind the lamp post and threw back the hood of her cape. Her hair shone gold in the pool of light as we looked at each other.

'Blimey, Lil,' she said. 'You don't half walk fast. You know I've only got little legs.'

'Lil…'
We were halfway through the foot
tunnel, at the point where the water above
was deepest and the echoes talked to each other
from both ends. You could tell it was the middle
because the passageway dipped slightly and then
started to climb again. When I was little and Dad
and I used to go and visit the cousins in Silvertown
on a Sunday, I used to run through the tunnel with
my football at my feet, and it would always roll to a
halt right at that magical centre point.

They'd built the tunnel just before the war so
the Arsenal workers didn't get stuck on the wrong
side of the river when it was too foggy for the ferry
boat, Dad told me. And ever since it opened

people had said there was something funny about it. The story was that time stopped down there, that you always came out the other side at exactly the same time you went in. Amy and I had tried to test it once, but we didn't have a watch, so we couldn't be sure and when I said I'd stay on our side and wave to her when she came out the other, she wouldn't do it because she was too scared to go down there on her own.

Amy had stopped suddenly and was looking at me. For a moment I thought she was going to tell me how well I'd played and how glad she was she'd come to the game, but this was Amy May. She wasn't interested in football.

'I wanted to say how sorry I am,' she said. I couldn't think what she meant at first. 'About what happened to your dad,' she added quickly. 'The accident, you know.'

I traced my finger along a crack in one of the tiles on the wall. 'Yeah,' I said. 'Thanks.' There was nothing else to say.

'Is that why . . . ?' She waggled a finger at my football kit.

'I joined Spurs?'

'Yeah. All the dressing-up-as-a-boy stuff.'

I shrugged. 'We needed the money.' My voice sounded very loud in the tunnel as I tried to make a joke of it. 'And they were hardly going to let me play as a girl.'

Amy didn't laugh. 'And the boy?' she said, after a small pause. 'The one with the legs who did all the running about?' She was trying to make it sound like she wasn't interested but I could tell she was.

'They've all got legs, Amy.'

'You know what I mean.' She took a deep breath. 'It's him, isn't it?' she said. The words came tumbling out quickly now. 'I didn't recognize him out of uniform at first, but then Billy told me his name and the penny dropped. It's your footballer pen pal, isn't it? Back from the front.'

I felt the familiar twang of jealousy in my chest. 'You should know,' I said. The words shot out of my mouth like bullets. 'You were the one who kissed him.' I walked on, my back stiff, my boots echoing in the silence.

'I knew it!' Amy's voice rang out from behind me bouncing off the sides of the tunnel. 'I knew it

I knew it I knew it! You were there, weren't you? That day at the zoo! You were blooming well there!'

I turned round slowly to look at her. She was hopping from foot to foot as if her body couldn't contain her delight.

'How did you know?' I said. 'I was . . .' I tried to find the right words, '. . . in disguise.' It sounded so silly when I put it like that.

'Oh for goodness' sake, Lil.' Amy stopped bouncing and walked towards me. 'We've been best friends since we were five years old. It'd take more than a pair of your dad's old trousers and a flat cap to hide from me, no matter how much you try and disappear behind lamp posts and sneak around pretending to be interested in crocodiles. Oh Lily, what are you like?' She reached out quickly and hugged me round the waist, resting her cheek on my chest, her whole body shaking with laughter. I found I had to swallow down a laugh myself. It wasn't easy to be angry with Amy May for long.

'I suppose it was a bit obvious,' I said.

'A bit! It was like you had a big sign on your head saying "I'm up to something!" I'm surprised the zookeepers didn't accuse you of trying to nick the penguins.'

She laughed again, looking up at me, and this time I let the laugh out and we laughed together just like we used to. Then I punched her shoulder and she kicked my leg and we walked on, Amy skipping beside me like a little girl.

'You didn't have to kiss him, though,' I said as we headed towards the stairs at the end of the tunnel.

Amy gave me one of her looks. 'Oh, but I did, Lil,' she said. 'I had no choice about that.'

'Why?'

She shrugged. 'I'd never kissed a boy before, had I? I wanted to know what it was like.'

'Wha-a-t? Hoy! Come back here!' Amy had started to scamper up the stairs, laughing as she ran. I clumped after her, my boots echoing in the gloom. 'Amy May, you baggage! You kissed your best friend's boy just to find out what it was like?'

Amy looked at me over her shoulder. 'Yup! And very nice it was too! You should try it sometime!'

'You!' I made a grab for her as we tumbled out into the night, laughing and tripping over each other's feet. And that was when she stopped and grabbed my arm.

'There's someone there, Lil. Look.'

I looked. A dark figure was standing in the shadows by the Arsenal wall, watching the exit from the tunnel. It was almost as if they were waiting for us.

'Who's there?' I called. 'What do you want?'

The figure stepped out of the shadows and stood in the light from a lamp post by the wall. A boat hooted on the river. The night smelt of soot and chemicals and mud, and my heart seemed to have stopped beating.

It was Jack.

Amy was the first to speak.

'Hello,' she said. 'What are you doing here?' Her voice sounded strange, sort of held back, as if it belonged to someone else.

Either Jack didn't remember her from the day at the zoo, or he didn't recognize her in the darkness. He just stood there, looking at me, still in his kit like me, still muddy from the game. Somewhere in a pub down the road, a woman laughed and a man started to sing.

'Why d'you do it, Charlie?' said Jack. 'I saw your

dad. He said you'd most likely come back this way.'

I opened my mouth but nothing came out. I didn't know what to say. Next to me, I felt Amy, standing very still, so close I could hear her breathing.

'How could you just walk away from the team like that?' Jack said. 'You're the best keeper we've ever had.'

There was a silence while my heart thudded in my ears. Suddenly Amy laughed. It was an odd high-pitched little sound that I'd never heard her make before. It frightened me, I don't know why.

'You mean he doesn't know?' she said. Her pretty face looked almost ugly in the half-light.

Jack took a step towards us. Behind him, the river was all black and silver, glittering with light. A young couple emerged from the tunnel and looked at us as they walked past.

'What?' Jack was still looking at me. 'What don't I know?'

Amy laughed again, waking some seagulls who flew up and drifted above us, ghostly grey shapes against the velvet black of the sky.

'I don't believe it!' Amy said, shaking her head in disbelief. 'You are wonderful! What a pair!'

A pair, I thought. *Is that what we are? A* pair? It didn't seem right.

'Amy—' I said. But Jack interrupted. He'd been staring at her, but now he turned to me.

'I don't understand,' he said. 'This is the girl I met at the zoo. Isn't it? The girl who said she was Lily, the girl I thought I'd been writing to.' Amy opened her mouth to speak, but he went on. 'Except it wasn't her. I knew it wasn't. But I liked her and I thought she liked me, but then, when I got back to the front, the letters stopped and Harry was killed and . . .' His face creased up and for one awful moment I thought he was going to cry. 'I didn't know what to do, Charlie,' he said. 'Nothing made sense any more. And now . . . it still doesn't.'

He reached out with one arm as if feeling for something to hold on to, to stop himself falling, but there was nothing there. Next to me, I felt Amy's body go tense as she drew herself to her full height. She was going to tell him. I knew she was.

'Amy,' I said. 'Please. Don't—'

'Amy?' Jack was looking at us both now. 'Is that her name?' Then: 'She's your sweetheart,' he said to me suddenly. 'You're engaged to be married.' He turned on Amy now, his face white and angry in the blue light from the street lamp. 'Is that why you stopped writing? Why didn't just say you had someone else? I would've understood.'

Amy took a deep breath. I knew she was going to tell him. And she did.

'Oh, you great fool, Jack Darling,' she said. 'How can you not see it?'

'See what?' he said. '*See what?*'

'She's a girl!'

He stared at me and opened his mouth then closed it again.

'This is Lily,' Amy went on. 'This is the girl who wrote to you. This is the girl whose letters got you through the war. This is your Lily Dodd!'

Nobody said anything.

'So go on,' said Amy. Her voice sounded high, like glass. 'Now you've found each other. Give her a kiss!'

Silence. My heart beating. The world swinging round the three of us, the seagulls wheeling pale against the sky, sounding like cats or babies, and Jack looking at us both through the lamplight.

And then, quite suddenly, Amy starting to cry.

Jack and I both made a move towards her and then stopped.

'Amy?' I said.

She made little fluttering movements with her hands to keep me away, then turned her face to me. It was all wet and shining with tears.

'I'm so sorry, Lil,' she said. 'I knew what you felt about him, but I couldn't help it. I thought it would be fun, a game, and then it stopped being a game and it was real and I'm so so so so sorry. I didn't mean it to happen, but it did and it has and I couldn't forget him even though you're my best friend and I never wanted to hurt you, Lily, I'd rather die.'

I looked from her to Jack and back to her and I knew she wasn't just talking about the kiss in the reptile house. It was more than that, much more.

'It's all right,' I said. Because in the moment I realized it was. Jack had been just an idea for me – a handsome face in a photograph, a football star, a dream of the perfect sweetheart. But that's all he was. A dream. Now we'd actually met we were pals, good pals, but no more than that. I felt myself smiling as I remembered what the crocodile had said: it was different for Jack and Amy. Deep down, I'd known it all along. So I said it again. 'Amy. It's all right.'

'It's not! It's not all right! It's horrible and I'm horrible and it hurts so much!'

'You're not horrible, Amy—' I held out my hand to her, but she backed away from it as if I was threatening her with a knife and then turned and started to run, back towards the tunnel.

'Go after her,' I said.

Jack looked at me, a question in his eyes.

'It's fine,' I said. 'Honestly, it really is.'

He stood there for a moment, while Amy's boots clanged down the steps.

'Go!' I said.

Jack hesitated, and then held out his hand. 'Thanks,' he said and then he gave a little grin. 'Charlie.'

I nodded. We shook hands and he turned and ran after Amy.

I stood there for a while, watching the boats. A man walked past, pushing some sort of barrow. He was whistling something, I don't know what. I could hear a woman scolding a child, and the sound of the hooter at the Arsenal calling the men into work for the night shift. Because they were men now, working in the factory, the women and girls had gone. And all round me the smell, the smell of the Arsenal mud and the Arsenal smoke and the Arsenal fog, so thick you could almost grab handfuls of it like snow. I felt cold in my shorts, but it didn't matter. Nothing seemed to matter much at all.

And then another voice. 'Lil?'

Billy Cracken was standing in a pool of lamplight with our little dog on his lead.

'Is everything all right? We were worried about you, me and your dad. I was worried about you. Lil?' His voice was trembling and everything fell into place. 'Are you all right?'

'Yes,' I said as I walked towards him. 'I'm absolutely fine.'

And then I took his hand and Billy Cracken and I folded into each other's arms and I kissed him and he kissed me and we kissed. And then, when we'd stopped kissing and I'd pulled away and laughed at his astonished face, I said, 'Come on, Bill. Let's go home.'

A FEW WEEKS LATER

'Lily! Lily of Laguna!'

It was a Sunday morning, the kind of bright spring day when strangers smile at each other in the street and the whole of London glitters in the sun. The war had been over for nearly four months, I'd got a job in a bakery while I was waiting to start at the women's college to train to be a teacher, and now I was back at the old Manor Ground playing football with my friends.

'Over here!'

'Jess!'

'To me, to me, to meeee!'

Most of us had lost our jobs. Some of us had lost our dads, our brothers, our sweethearts. But we still had each other. We still had the Rockets.

It was Miss Barker, the lady supervisor from the Arsenal, who'd encouraged us to keep playing. 'I'm not having it,' she'd said. 'No, girls, I'm really not having it, not after all your hard work. You might not work at the Arsenal any more, but you're still the Rockets.'

So we'd carried on training on the common, and then Miss Barker had found out that the Nippies were still playing, so she'd organized another game, this time without Joe Crawford sneering at us from the side of the pitch. And so here I was, back in my old kit, standing in my goal with my friends in front of me and my dad on the touchline with Wilfred and my own Billy Cracken at his side. Amy was there too, eating peanuts and looking very small between her two brothers back from the war. She never went up to White Hart Lane to see Jack play, because as she said, he had plenty of people to watch him, the big-head, he didn't need her there as well – and anyway, she'd never known how interesting football could be until she saw it being played by girls.

'Lily! Lily Dodd!' It was Jess. The Nippies' centre-forward was pelting towards my goal, ghosting through the defence, the ball at her feet, effortless.

Watch the player, I thought, *not the ball.*

I watched her. Peggy went in for a tackle but the forward just skipped past her. The ball looked as if it was glued to her feet.

'Defence! Get back!'

She was good, this girl, I thought, as good as Jess, better maybe. She wasn't as strong and determined, but she was faster, there was a joy in the way she played that made her fun to watch. But there was no way she was going to get that ball past me. I made myself big, so big that I filled the whole goal. And I waited, on my own but part of the team. The keeper.

'Get back!' Jess was shouting. 'Rockets! Get back there and support your keeper! ROCKETS!'

The girl with the ball looked up as she homed in on my goal. Our eyes locked and for a moment it felt like there was nobody in the world except us. The shouts of the other girls faded away and there was just her and me and the ball, with the sky hanging blue above us and the grass beneath our boots. And then she dropped her left shoulder, drew back her right leg and . . .

BOOF!

The ball came flying towards my goal, a high swinging shot, heading for the top right corner. I knew exactly where it was going and I knew exactly what I was going to do.

I did what I did best.

I jumped.

HOW IT BEGAN

When I was growing up, I went to a very small secondary school in Suffolk where the girls played hockey in winter, tennis in summer, and sometimes, when it rained, had to stay indoors and do something called Country Dancing. I liked hockey, hated tennis and got thrown out of country dancing for not taking it seriously. Then, one day, we asked the PE teacher if we could play football like the boys.

No, she said. Football was not suitable for girls, it was too physical, we could get hurt.

We didn't understand. How were we more likely to get hurt playing football than hockey, with its hefty wooden sticks and rock-hard ball that came hurtling through the air at a hundred miles an hour? We were constantly getting our shins and ankles whacked to pieces and the only protection for the goalkeeper was a pair of ill-fitting cricket pads strapped to her poor cold legs. But that was that. Football was Not For Girls.

We knew it wasn't true. We knew that girls had always kicked balls around in parks and playgrounds just like their brothers. What we didn't know was that there was a time when they played the game seriously. A time when they formed their own teams and leagues and played on some of the most famous grounds in the country, often in front of bigger crowds than the men's professional teams.

It started in 1914, at the beginning of World War One. When the men and boys went away to fight, women and girls took their places in the munitions factories, making the bombs and bullets that were needed to win the war. They became known as munitionettes, and for many of them it was the first time they were able to earn their own living, spend time away from their families, and, of course, play football. All over Britain, female factory workers started to form their own teams and organize matches for charity. At first it was seen as a novelty, a bit of a laugh, to go along and watch a load of girls kicking a ball about, but gradually people started to realize the girls could really play, and more and more people started to go to the matches. Then in 1915, when the Football Association suspended the professional men's game for the duration of the war, the girls started to play on their grounds, attracting crowds as big as – and sometimes bigger than – the men. The most successful team of all, the Dick, Kerr Ladies from Preston (the comma isn't a typo – it was originally a team of workers from a factory owned by a Mr Dick and a Mr Kerr), drew huge crowds. The biggest was 53,000 people inside the ground with over 14,000 locked out – a record for a women's match that wasn't beaten until the 2012 Olympics when England played Brazil. Ladies' football was a success.

So what happened?

Well, the war ended. The men and boys needed their jobs back. The women and girls got kicked out of the factories. And the gentlemen of the Football Association decided they didn't like the idea of females playing football after all, so in 1921 they made their announcement:

'Complaints having been made as to football being played by women, the Council feel impelled to express their strong opinion that the game of football is quite unsuitable for females and ought not to be encouraged.'

They went on to say that they would expel any club who allowed ladies' teams to play on their grounds.

And that was that. Some teams in the north of England continued to play on rugby league grounds, but most disbanded. The days when women's football attracted crowds of over 50,000 people were over.

Of course, my friends and I didn't know any of this when we asked our PE teacher if we could play football, and the first time I heard about it was only a few years ago when my friend Tony wrote a show featuring a very tall lady footballer called Gerty Naylor. I was intrigued, and started to read about the women and girls that went into the factories during the war and formed their own football teams.

And that's when I found out about the Rockets.

Although the Royal Arsenal in Woolwich was the biggest munitions factory in the country, and its men's football team went on to become one of the most famous in the world, not much is known about their ladies' team. I don't know if they ever played the Lyons' Corner House Ladies, and I don't expect they had a very tall goalkeeper who went on to play for Spurs. My Lily Dodd might not have existed, but there were lots of other Lilys (and Jesses and Peggys and Pollys) who did. In fact, I borrowed my Lily's name from a Lily that some people think was the greatest female player of all time.

Lily Parr started playing for Dick, Kerr's Ladies when she was only fourteen. She scored forty-three goals in her first season, and went on to score nearly a thousand in her playing career. Like my Lily, Lily Parr was a tall girl, nearly six feet, who was said to have a harder shot that most male players. One of her teammates wrote that she'd never seen any woman—'nor any man' – kick a ball like Lily. When a professional male goalkeeper challenged Lily to get a shot past him, she accepted and went on, not just to score, but to break his arm with the power of her shot. So I didn't just borrow Lily Parr's name; I borrowed a story about her. I don't think she'd mind.

Lily Parr didn't stop playing football when the FA banned the women's game. She went on to play for Preston Ladies until she was forty-five and lived long enough to see the day in 1971, fifty years after the original announcement, when the Football Association finally lifted the ban on women's football.

When I said that many people think Lily Parr was the greatest female player of all time, I should've added two words. So. Far.

Lily Parr was the greatest female player in the world so far.

Now it's your turn.